Suddenly, Jen pointed at [illegible]ahead.

At first, Sam saw a wavering pool of light. She couldn't have said whether it was silver or gold, water or molten metal. She only knew the flash hurt her eyes with its brilliance. A village was turned upside down in the midst of it.

Talk about impossible! She blinked and squinted. That splash of radiance was pretty far off. She focused hard. No, it wasn't that far away. Perhaps a mile.

For a second, Sam told herself she should have eaten breakfast before she rode out this morning. Gram always said Sam's brain would work better if she ate.

But hunger and distance couldn't explain what she saw next.

Fairy light and golden, a palomino horse flickered across the playa, danced through a row of upside-down houses — and vanished.

*Read all the books in the* PHANTOM STALLION *series:*

∾ 1 ∾
THE WILD ONE

∾ 2 ∾
MUSTANG MOON

∾ 3 ∾
DARK SUNSHINE

∾ 4 ∾
THE RENEGADE

∾ 5 ∾
FREE AGAIN

∾ 6 ∾
THE CHALLENGER

∾ 7 ∾
DESERT DANCER

∾ 8 ∾
GOLDEN GHOST

# Phantom Stallion

## ◅◦ 8 ◦▻

## Golden Ghost

TERRI FARLEY

**AVON BOOKS**

*An Imprint of HarperCollinsPublishers*

Library of Congress Catalog Card Number:
2003090448
ISBN 0-06-053726-4

First Avon edition, 2003

Visit us on the World Wide Web!
www.harperchildrens.com

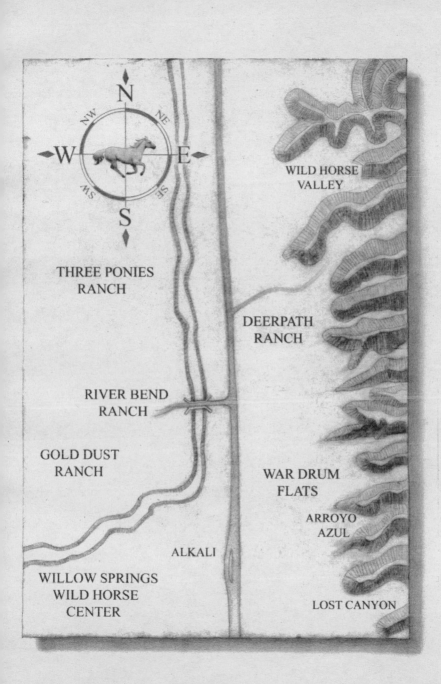

## Chapter One

**M**anes lashing, forelegs reaching, two horses galloped side by side across the high desert of Nevada. The palomino and the bay drank in crisp January air as they strained against their reins. They rejoiced in the dazzling blue and white day just as much as their riders.

Samantha Forster leaned low on Ace's neck. Her eyes squinted almost shut as the bay ran into the wind. If she hadn't pulled her hair into a tight clip under her old brown Stetson, it would be blizzarding around her face. On days like this, when he'd left the warm confinement of the barn behind, Ace's surging eagerness reminded her he was a mustang.

The bay gelding longed to run with a herd, even

if it was only a herd of two. A sudden tug at the bit telegraphed along the reins into Sam's hands. Her fingers closed tighter and her deerskin gloves kept the reins from sliding away.

Ace wanted to race. Although Jen's big palomino mare, Silk Stockings, was sixteen hands to his fourteen, Ace always thought he could win. Once in a while he could, when the palomino turned skittish and proved Jen's insight in nicknaming her mare Silly.

Sam turned her head just enough to see Jen.

Jen leaned slightly forward in her saddle. Her white-blond braids streamed behind her, flat on the wind, and morning sunlight glazed the lenses of her glasses. Jen didn't notice Sam's glance. She rode like a female Paul Revere, as if she had a mission and only her palomino mare could take her there.

Jennifer Kenworthy was Sam's best friend and she'd been gone for most of winter vacation. But Jen and her mom had driven in from Utah late the night before.

Even though it had been nearly eleven, long past Sam's nine o'clock limit on phone calls, Jen had braved Dad's anger and called Sam to beg for an early-morning ride. Jen's desperation meant her parents hadn't reached a truce.

Maybe because Dad had just returned from his honeymoon, or because Brynna, his new wife, reminded him it was, after all, vacation, Dad allowed

Sam to talk with Jen, and make plans to meet between River Bend and Gold Dust ranches, for a ride.

This morning, Sam had dressed in the dark. She'd pulled on the jeans, red pullover sweater, and boots she'd laid out the night before, then tiptoed downstairs without squeaking a single board.

She even made it out to the barn without Blaze, River Bend Ranch's watchdog, raising a ruckus.

Sam couldn't think of anything better than celebrating Jen's first day back with a run across War Drum Flats.

Sure, they watched for cracks and bare roots, anything that meant disaster if a horse tripped at a full run, but they knew this patch of alkali desert well. It spread before them in all directions, smooth and level as a white tablecloth.

For a few steps, Ace veered east. Sam corrected him, keeping him in step with Silly, but her heart pulled toward the Calico Mountains just as Ace's did.

From the corner of her eye, Sam could just see the mountain range. Glowing in the morning sun, the peaks looked smooth and soft, as if they'd been molded from orange sherbet. But things weren't always what they seemed. The peaks were inaccessible to cars or trucks and only the most determined rider could follow the faint paths etched by deer, antelope, and wild horses.

The Calico Mountains were steep and dangerous and Sam was glad.

She'd seen the Phantom scale that rocky mountain face just a few days ago. He and his new lead mare had been guiding his herd back into their secret valley. They were there now, Sam thought with a sigh, safe for the winter. She had no reason to worry over the great silver stallion.

Everything in her own life was fine, too. Even though she had a brand-new stepmother, Sam trusted Brynna Olson—now Forster—to fit into the family.

Tranquility for the mustangs and her family meant Sam could single-mindedly attack her goal for the three days until school recommenced: she'd help Jen.

With a squeal of frustration, Ace surged forward. He wanted to run faster than his short legs would carry him.

Beyond the thunder of running hooves and the wind singing through Ace's mane, Sam heard the slapping of her saddlebags. Each time Ace's hind legs shot behind him, leather creaked. The pouches, buckled to her saddle, hung heavy with schoolwork and a flashlight.

Jen had arrived home just in time. There were three days until the end of vacation. Three days until they had to turn in the first stage of their homework on the ghost town of Nugget.

"No problem," Sam muttered to Ace, "except we haven't seen it yet."

Since she was a little kid, Sam had heard stories

about the old mining town of Nugget. At night, little white lights appeared in the old general store, said one tale, and the saloon had a trapdoor that dropped into black nothingness. The ground which the town sat on was supposed to be unstable, because it sat above miles of earth honeycombed with mine shafts. Those were supposed to be filled with poisonous gases and, of course, the entire town of Nugget was rumored to be haunted.

Why hadn't she ever been there? Until ten years ago, the town hadn't even been locked up. Now, while it awaited status as a historic landmark, a padlocked gate blocked the entrance. According to Mrs. Ely, only one team of students would receive a key to that padlock.

Sam felt her own satisfied smile. That key was in her pocket.

When Mrs. Ely had posted a list of term project ideas on the bulletin board, she'd mentioned they could partner with a student from another one of her classes. Sam had sprinted from her seat to the bulletin board and been first in line to sign up for that key to Nugget.

She knew Jen would jump at the chance to explore the nearby ghost town, on horseback, so she wrote down Jen's name as her partner.

"Hey!" Jen sat back in her saddle, pulling Sam's thoughts back to the present.

Silly's head swung from side to side, looking for

danger. Finding none, she slowed, in response to her rider's request.

When Ace pretended he hadn't noticed, Sam shortened her reins. Ace's neck bowed at the crest as Sam pulled in even more, but his gallop stayed smooth and fast.

"Oh quit it," she scolded her horse. Then, she added, "You're tired, boy. You just don't know it yet."

For a few seconds, Ace seemed to run in place beneath her. Finally, with a snort and a toss of his head, he slowed to a hammering trot.

"Ow, ow, ow," Sam complained.

She couldn't quite match her seat to his gait. Every inch of her spine felt Ace's hooves hammering on the playa. Ace usually slowed to a lope, a gentle jog, and then a walk. He could do it with fluid smoothness, but he'd decided to make her teeth crack together.

"Is this your way of getting even?" she asked him as they finally came even with Silly and Jen.

"Me?" Jen asked. She blinked owlishly behind her glasses and held her reins in her left hand as she flattened her right palm to her chest.

"Of course, not you." Sam laughed, relieved Ace had finally slowed to a walk.

"What was I thinking?" Jen rolled her eyes. "Interrupting your conversation with your horse."

Sam stuck out her tongue, knowing Jen wasn't

the least bit offended. Jen planned to become a veterinarian, and she was always trying to psych out her own horse.

"Really, though," Jen said, sighing as Silly and Ace matched steps in a flat-footed walk. "I'm sorry I delayed us."

"Like I would have started my homework last week, anyway," Sam said, dismissing Jen's apology. "With Dad, Brynna, and Gram gone, and Aunt Sue here instead, it was a weeklong party. We stayed up late, ate junk food, and watched movies. I didn't even think about homework."

"I always think about homework," Jen said.

"That's why you get all A's and I'm happy with B's."

"Not on this project," Jen cautioned her. "This counts for a grade in science, English, and history, so there's no way we can settle for a B."

Sam grimaced. Jen was right. They needed to do extra great work on this project.

"You could get all A's if you wanted to. You know that, don't you?"

"You sound like Dad and Gram," Sam muttered.

"You mean Brynna hasn't started in on you yet?" Jen asked slyly. "She will."

"Don't make me put my hands over my ears," Sam begged. "My horse will run away with me and then we'll be another day behind on this project."

They rode in silence for a few minutes. Sam looked around, wishing there were shrubs or trees to tell her if there was a faint breeze blowing. Currents of warmth seemed to flow through the cold air. Sam didn't think she was imagining it, but it didn't make much sense.

"This first part of the project will be a piece of cake," Jen said. "All we have to do is look for artifacts. How hard can that be?"

Sam shrugged.

Artifacts, Mrs. Ely had explained, could be all kinds of stuff. Frying pans, buttons, horseshoe nails, hatpins, toys, and even tin cans counted, if they were old enough. But since Sam didn't know how or why Nugget had become a ghost town, she couldn't imagine people leaving lots of stuff behind.

"Did they have to leave in a hurry?" Sam asked.

Still feeling feisty, Ace pretended to nip at Silly's neck. The palomino shied, but Jen kept her under control.

"What?" Jen asked. "Did who leave in a hurry?"

"The people who lived in Nugget, of course. Why did it turn into a ghost town instead of hanging in there like Darton, or even Alkali?"

"Got me," Jen said. She rubbed Silly's neck, comforting her, though the mare knew she had nothing to fear from Ace. "Really, considering how close it is, I can't believe we haven't gone exploring there before."

"Why haven't we?" Sam asked.

"Other than the fact that it's closed to the public?" Jen shrugged.

Sam couldn't believe Jen didn't offer a theory, even if she wasn't sure it was true. Jennifer Kenworthy had an opinion about everything.

"Probably the gold ran out, don't you think?" Sam asked.

"That'd be the logical explanation," Jen said. "But what if it was something else?"

"Like what?" Sam asked, but she didn't want to know. Not if it was something creepy.

"Outlaws nearby?" Jen suggested. "Or a plague?"

"Right," Sam agreed. "Or they could've been chased down the main street by a pack of rabid wolves."

"My ideas aren't *that* far-fetched," Jen insisted.

Cold wind picked up a lock of Ace's mane and waved it. The sudden cold chilled Sam and she didn't know if she was eager or reluctant to get into the canyon that held Nugget. It should be warmer, sheltered from the wind, but she felt kind of safe out here on the playa, where she could see everything. Once they turned left into the canyon, they'd be out of sight of the road and any other riders who happened by.

"Plague isn't illogical?" Sam asked. She pretended to hold a telephone receiver to her ear. "Hello, frontier doctor? Sorry to bother you, but we have a case of the Black Death over here—"

"There are a few historical problems with what you just said," Jen told her. "You realize that, right? But there was bubonic plague down in the mines. The miners took along lunch pails, and left behind crumbs, and then the rats—"

"Remind me not to go into the mines while we're in Nugget," Sam interrupted.

"Mine shafts aren't exactly my favorite places to begin with," Jen said. "Besides, my dad says Nugget is haunted."

"I was really hoping you wouldn't say that." Sam moaned.

"Why? Neither of us believes it's true."

Sam felt a hum of tension along her nerves. Of course it wasn't true, but why had Jen even brought it up?

"I can promise you that's not the reason I've never been here," Sam said. "My dad doesn't believe in anything he can't see, touch, smell, or taste."

"You left something out," Jen said. "How about hearing? Doesn't he trust what he hears?"

"Nope," Sam said. "Too easy to get fooled."

Just then, a high-pitched sound made both horses stop.

Silly froze, ears pricked straight and trembling.

"What was that?" Sam said quietly.

"A bird?" Jen offered.

"But it sounded like—" Sam began. She closed her lips. It sounded like a flute. A bone flute of the sort used in Native American ceremonies. But that was impossible.

Suddenly, Jen pointed and Sam looked ahead.

At first, Sam saw a wavering pool of light. She couldn't have said whether it was silver or gold, water or molten metal. She only knew the flash hurt her eyes with its brilliance. A village was turned upside down in the midst of it.

Talk about impossible! She blinked and squinted. That splash of radiance was pretty far off. She focused hard. No, it wasn't that far away. Perhaps a mile.

For a second, Sam told herself she should have eaten breakfast before she rode out this morning. Gram always said Sam's brain would work better if she ate.

But hunger and distance couldn't explain what she saw next.

Fairy light and golden, a palomino horse flickered across the playa, danced through a row of upside-down houses — and vanished.

# Chapter Two

$\mathcal{J}$ust ahead, after the turnoff to Lost Canyon but before the trail to Nugget, the houses remained on their roofs, afloat in a sea of glittering water.

"It's a mirage, of course," Jen said slowly as the horses moved forward again. "But wow, I've never seen anything like it."

*A mirage.*

Sam's shoulders sagged with relief. Mirages weren't mystical. You saw mirages in cartoons.

Even though the Saturday mornings she finished her chores early and slipped into the living room to sprawl on the couch were rare, she remembered seeing cartoons in which a guy—or was it a rabbit?—crawled across a killing-hot desert toward an imagined oasis. Pretty soon he'd be drinking sand as if it were the sweetest, clearest water on the planet.

But it was January. They'd ridden through some warm currents of air getting here, but it couldn't be called hot. Juniper grew here, and piñon pines. This wasn't the Sahara Desert. Or a cartoon.

Ace stopped so suddenly, Sam almost fell off.

She wished he'd done it a few minutes ago, before the golden horse vanished. That would have meant he'd seen it, too. And she'd be sure it wasn't her imagination.

She wanted to ask Jen if she'd seen the horse, but she just couldn't.

On the other hand, Jen had seen something, or she wouldn't have mentioned the mirage. But maybe houses standing on their heads were enough to astound Jen.

Sam stared hard. She knew what was real and what wasn't. Ahead, there was nothing but the trail to Lost Canyon. Beyond it, there was an even fainter trail, as if someone had dragged an eraser across the desert floor.

"It's not Nugget," Sam said, trying to nudge Jen to explain.

"Of course not," Jen snapped.

Sam knew Jen too well to take offense at her tone. In fact, Jen's irritation was sort of amusing. She couldn't chuckle, of course, or even smile. But her best friend, who was so good at math, science, and every other logical thing, was thrown off balance by the image shimmering before them.

"That's just a mirage, as I said."

*Of what?* Sam wanted to know, but she didn't ask.

Ace dropped his head and sniffed the alkali dust

beneath his hooves. Silly did the same. They passed the time until their riders decided what to do next.

Sam decided she wasn't much different from the horses. She waited, letting Jen figure things out.

As the only freshman reporter on the school newspaper, Sam knew she was good with words. She could report on this mirage, but she'd leave it up to Jen to figure it out.

"Well, of course it's not Nugget," Jen said. She pointed and her lips were set in a hard line, but she sounded like she was convincing herself. "Look, there. See that thing? It's like—" Jen broke off, shaking her head. "It looks like a traffic light, doesn't it?"

"It does," Sam agreed. "I know it's a mirage," she added. "And I know it's not really there, but how do mirages work?"

"There's nothing supernatural about them," Jen said. "It has to do with atmospheric refraction. I remember reading that there are either multiple or inverted images. So, that fits."

"But where *is* that?" Sam asked. "The place, I mean. Where's it from?"

"I don't know," Jen admitted. "Do you suppose my biology teacher would think I was kissing up if I called him and asked? Wherever it is, it's not upside down. I know that much."

"If we ride right at it, will it disappear or move away? Or maybe," Sam said, feeling a shiver, "we can ride through it."

"I *think* it will vanish," Jen said, gathering her reins. "But I don't really know. Shall we test my theory?"

They loped toward Nugget. Before them, the image faded and finally disappeared. Sam didn't see so much as a flicker of the golden horse.

No road or trail led into Nugget, but Mrs. Ely had told them how to find the path.

"There's the gate," Jen said. She pointed to a big iron gate, painted chrome yellow. A padlock the size of Sam's fist kept it closed. "You've got the key, right?"

Sam retrieved it from her saddlebag, dismounted, and gave the key a try. It opened smoothly and perfectly.

"After you," Sam said.

She let Jen ride ahead of her, then led Ace through. When they were both on the Nugget side of the gate, Sam relocked it and slipped the key into her pocket. Then she remounted Ace.

Sam bit her lip as Ace picked his way over the tumble of rocks and dirt that marked the way to the abandoned town.

"Careful, girl," Jen cautioned Silly as her hooves grated on a boulder that tilted as she stepped on it.

Mrs. Ely had said the path stretched for about a mile, but it seemed longer.

When Jen drew rein beside her, Sam noticed

Silly showed dark patches of sweat. The mare tugged at her bit with foam-flecked lips.

Ace was quieter than usual. The horses were tired and glad when the path smoothed into a dirt road.

The ghost town stood before them, gray and eerie as an empty movie set.

"Now we know why we weren't allowed to come here before," Jen said.

Sam swept a frightened glance around the ghost town before she said, "You mean the rough ride to get here?"

"Sure I do," Jen said, but the sarcastic edge to her voice told Sam that Jen felt the menacing atmosphere, too.

A line of shacks huddled shoulder to shoulder on the left side of the main street. Actually, Sam thought, looking around, it was the only street.

A few hitching rails and water troughs stood before the faltering buildings, but no one had built boardwalks to keep the skirts of Western ladies from brushing the mud. This place had been built and abandoned in a hurry.

Sam studied the buildings. Some were shops and some homes, but all had weathered to the same gray color and they slanted at the same angle, pushed halfway down by the high desert wind.

"There was a crooked man and he had a crooked house," Jen recited in a singsong voice.

"Stop it," Sam hissed. "It was just built in a hurry. They found gold and wanted to get in out of the weather and these were better than tents."

Sam couldn't have explained why the nursery rhyme creeped her out, or why she was whispering.

On the right side of the dirt street, a row of wind-bent piñon pines ringed a slightly larger shack. A wooden rectangle supported a tarnished bell with a short, frayed rope.

The school, Sam guessed. Even though the town had only existed for a couple of years, there must have been children here, and a teacher. Behind it was an open area and then a ravine.

Had that ravine been blasted by dynamite or fissured open by an earthquake? It went so far back into the hill, you could almost call it a canyon. She'd bet someone who knew geology would say it had been "born by violence." The hillside had been cracked open like an egg.

The street slanted upward, then ended in a graveyard full of grave markers. They zigzagged in uneven rows across the face of a small hill.

Wind gusted. The horses pricked their ears as a tumbleweed battered against the graveyard fence, trying to get out. Then, there was a *creeeak* sound, followed by a slam, and both horses shied.

Sam saw a shutter on the schoolhouse move. Ace jumped sideways, bumping into Silly.

"It's only the wind," Jen said soothingly, as Silly swished her tail and shivered. "What's got you all skittish?"

"As if you don't know," Sam muttered. She rode

Ace in a circle to distract him from Silly's fit of nerves. "This place is weird."

"It's not so weird." Jen gave a soft laugh and stroked her mare's damp neck. "Let's ride to the end of the road—"

"I'm not going into that graveyard," Sam interrupted. "Not yet, I mean."

"Don't tell me you've turned superstitious?" Jen joked. "Besides, I just meant it might settle the horses to let them sniff around a little."

Sam decided it might be an okay idea. When Jen urged Silly forward, she let Ace follow.

The horses' hooves crunched as they passed the buildings. Sam was surprised to see she could make out faded letters on some of them.

*General Store.* Sam wondered if there was anything left inside. Canned goods? Bolts of calico cloth? Maybe big wooden barrels used to hold pickles or crackers for a miner's lunch?

*Assay Office.*

"Hey," Sam said, pointing. "Isn't an assay office the place miners went to have their gold ore weighed? I bet they traded it in for money, too."

"Are you thinking there are silver coins or antique dollar bills, maybe even a little gold dust still inside?" Jen teased.

"It's possible," Sam said.

"Old treasures are always guarded by ghosts," Jen warned in a wavering voice.

"Be quiet," Sam told her automatically.

But Sam's uneasiness had just about disappeared and she went back to studying the faded buildings.

*Sheriff* was written in scrolled lettering that had once been black. That little office looked straighter and sturdier than the rest. Maybe there was a jail inside and the structure had been built to withstand vigilantes set on hanging outlaws who weren't convicted fast enough.

Sam felt herself smiling. This really was sort of cool. Every Western movie she'd seen came flooding back, with embellishments from her imagination.

*Ice.* That was sort of strange. Wouldn't ice be a luxury in a little desert town?

*Battle-Born Saloon.* Sam turned the name over in her mind, remembering Nevada had become a state during the Civil War.

She leaned forward in the saddle, trying to see through the open front of the structure. Though that rectangle on the saloon's street side had been empty for decades, it looked as if the saloon might have been the only place with glass windows. They must have been expensive in those days.

She pictured an old horse-drawn wagon coming down that steep and rocky road she and Jen had just traveled. Carrying a piece of glass had to have been delicate, risky work.

"What do we do besides collect artifacts?" Jen asked, when they'd passed the school and were almost to the graveyard. "I haven't had a chance to look at the assignment since I got back."

Sam had reread Mrs. Ely's handout just last night and she had no trouble remembering the assignment. For once, she was ahead of Jen.

"First, we take field notes," Sam said.

She figured that meant writing down what they observed. A suspicious scuff on the dirt road reminded her to watch for hoof prints.

She was sure she had *not* imagined the gold horse in the midst of that mirage. What if it had jumped the locked yellow gate then run down Nugget's main street? Or maybe it had followed a secret trail that led around the gate.

Sam listened for the sound of a brook or stream. She only heard the wind's low moan as it chased its tail around the old gray buildings. But if there'd been a town here, there had to be a source of water.

Sam looked up at the canyon walls. They'd block the worst of the wind. With water, shelter, and a bounty of weeds to eat, a lone horse could stay here quite comfortably.

"What else do we have to do, besides the field notes?" Jen asked.

She sounded a little irritated. Clearly, she'd noticed Sam wasn't paying attention to the conversation about the project.

"Mapping, cataloguing, and writing a report comparing this ghost town with a contemporary town. I think that's all," Sam said.

And then she saw them.

Unlike her friend Jake, Sam was no tracker. But here, the alkali dust showed clear hoof imprints. If they'd been old, they would have blown away, so they must be very recent. That was all the evidence Sam needed to believe a real bone-and-blood horse had walked here.

"With two of us, that shouldn't be very hard," Jen said.

Sam looked up. What could Jen be talking about?

"What are you staring at on the ground?" Jen blurted. "You're hanging halfway out of your saddle!"

"I'm looking for stuff to put in our field notes!" Sam replied angrily.

Jen's surprised stare told Sam she'd overreacted to Jen's question.

"What did I say?" Jen asked, dodging Silly's head as the mare reacted with alarm at Sam's voice. "Sor-*ry*. Don't tell me, if it's that big a deal."

"I'll tell you, but you're not allowed to make fun of me."

"When do I ever make fun of you?"

"Only all the time," Sam told her. "Don't pretend your feelings are all hurt, either, Jennifer Kenworthy. Remember when you told me I was anthro—" Sam stopped. "Anthro . . ." Now she was really mad. Why couldn't she remember that stupid word?

"Anthropomorphizing?" Jen asked calmly. "Giving human traits to animals?"

"Right," Sam said with a nod. "You said I was doing that to the Phantom."

"And you were. You always do, because you love him." Jen pushed her wire-framed glasses up on her nose.

Suddenly, Ace and Silly stopped, legs braced. They snorted in surprise.

*The tumbleweed*, Sam thought. *Here it comes*.

Wind had finally pushed the tumbleweed through the cemetery gate. On the loose, a stickery weed, big as a calf, bounded toward them.

But Ace and Silly weren't watching the tumble-weed. They gazed toward the schoolhouse.

The tremulous, high-pitched neigh lasted only an instant.

"Look!" Jen gasped while Sam was still staring.

Flame gold, the horse peered around a corner of the schoolhouse. Cream mane tangled to her shoulder. Curve-tipped ears and a dainty muzzle pointed toward them. When her head tilted to one side, considering them from another angle, her forelock parted over chocolate eyes. A loud sniff told the horse they were strangers. Furrows appeared over her eyes. Fear made her forefeet dance in place, tapping the hard ground.

It all happened in seconds, and then the horse was gone.

"Wait!" Jen pleaded, but she didn't wait to see if the horse stopped.

Together, the girls urged their mounts forward. The horses lunged with eagerness. Keen on following the palomino, they didn't seem to notice that their shoulders bumped as they took the turn around the schoolhouse.

Years of windblown dust hid stone paths through the schoolhouse garden. Ace's shod hooves slipped on rock. He didn't go down, but he slowed.

"The ravine!" Jen shouted, and sent Silly after the other palomino.

One closeup look at the ravine told Sam that Jen's pursuit wouldn't last long. Red-orange layers of earth had settled over purplish dirt. Though the place was barren, Sam heard the sound of water flowing around heaps of rocks.

Jen wasn't foolish enough to risk her horse's delicate legs in that boulder-strewn trap. No way.

But Jen kept riding. With tight-legged insistence, she pushed Silly on.

There must be a path through the rocks, Sam thought. She just couldn't see it from here. After all, the strange palomino had disappeared right through there, and she was no ghost.

Silly couldn't find a trail, at least not at a gallop. Her ears flicked in all directions and she squealed in frustration, trying to follow her rider's orders.

Jen looked frantically from one side of her mount's neck to the other, but then she seemed to give up. She sagged back in the saddle. Obviously she couldn't find the path, either.

Sam was glad. She'd never seen Jen ride with such recklessness.

Silly gave a choked neigh. Was she caught? A hoof could easily lodge between rocks. But then Jen's voice came over the clatter of the mare's hooves.

"Okay," Jen comforted. "Okay, girl. You did a great job, but she's gone."

Looking over her shoulder, Jen backed Silly, step by step, out of the ravine. She didn't wheel the mare until she'd reached the almost-level schoolhouse garden. When Jen swung Silly around at last, Sam was amazed at her friend's joyous smile.

Wind clanged the school bell in noisy celebration. Silly pranced like a parade horse, and the braid hanging over Jen's shoulder, straight with a tassel on the end, looked like an exclamation mark.

"We found treasure after all," Jen whooped. "And it's not some ordinary bag of gold. It's Rosa d'Oro, the lost Kenworthy palomino, alive as she can be!"

## Chapter Three

No wonder Jen had abandoned her usual good sense.

"That was her," Jen insisted, as they dismounted in front of the sheriff's office to let the horses drink from a wooden trough of rainwater. "I'm positive."

As Jen stared dreamily toward the ravine, Sam tried to recall what she'd heard about the Kenworthy palominos.

For decades, Jen's family had owned the Diamond K Ranch, and they'd been famous for their palominos. When years of drought had forced the Kenworthys to raise money or lose the ranch, they'd sold off the golden horses, one by one.

Even that hadn't been enough to save the Diamond K. When only five palominos remained, Jen's parents had had no choice but to sell the ranch. The buyer with the best offer had been Linc Slocum.

Linc Slocum had made a fortune through shady

deals and wild schemes that worked just often enough to keep him a millionaire. Since his arrival in Nevada, he'd used his money and toothpaste-commercial smile to buy the life of a Hollywood cowboy.

The Kenworthys' ranch had become part of his Wild West fantasy. And every ranch needed a weathered, no-nonsense foreman. Jed Kenworthy, a lifelong rancher with eyes that drooped like a bassett hound's, fit Linc Slocum's image of a foreman. So, even though Slocum had changed Diamond K into the Gold Dust Ranch, he'd kept Jed Kenworthy on to boss the cattle and cowboys.

That was what made Slocum's offer the best, Sam figured. Jen's family had stayed right at home.

But Sam didn't remember hearing any stories of a horse with a Spanish name.

"Tell me what happened again," Sam urged. "And what was the horse's name?"

"Rosa d'Oro. 'Golden Rose' is the translation. But there's not much to tell," Jen said.

"How can you say that? If this really is her—"

"Yeah, I know," Jen said. Her face lit up and she hugged her ribs with delight. "But no one knows what happened, exactly." Jen shook her head, then launched into a story. "Dad kept five horses—Golden Champagne, Sonora Sundance, Silk Stockings, Mantilla, and Golden Rose—two stallions and three mares, just in case he could get the breeding farm up and running again. But his idea fizzled, big time. He knew Mom's mare, Mantilla, might not make a brood mare, because she was too old, but Silly was a disappointment," Jen's voice softened and she petted her palomino as the mare rubbed her damp muzzle on Jen's shoulder.

Sam tried to think of Silly as Silk Stockings. The sixteen-hand palomino Quarter horse had flashy white stockings and near-perfect conformation. How could she be a disappointment?

"She's infertile," Jen explained. "Even though she's been bred a dozen times, she never gets pregnant. And then when Linc bought Champ, he insisted on having him gelded, so that put him out of the breeding program."

"Slocum doesn't deserve him," Sam said.

Why had Jed Kenworthy sold Champ to Linc Slocum? The rich man wasn't much of a rider. Champ's temperament and training were wasted on him. Slocum saw the palomino as just another pretty toy.

"Dad knew that, but Slocum traded the house for Champ," Jen explained. "We don't have to pay rent or anything. He traded us straight across."

"Wow." Sam gasped. A horse for a house. Was any horse worth that much money?

"So that left Sundance and Rose for breeding stock." Jen held up her hand, folded down three fingers and left two upright. "Dad bought Rose from a ranch in Mexico. Her bloodlines went back to conquistadors' horses brought from Spain hundreds of years ago. She was the Moorish type of palomino Queen Isabella liked. You know, Queen Isabella who gave Christopher Columbus his money?"

Sam nodded, but asked, "Moorish?"

"She had the black skin and delicate face of an Arabian and she was a golden butterscotch color." Grinning, Jen pointed toward the ravine. "I didn't get a great look at her, but from what I remember, that horse could be her twin.

"Anyway, Dad got her just before things went bad. I remember Mom didn't want to spend the money because Rose was just a two-year-old and they had to wait for her to mature before they could show or breed her."

"So, your family called her Rose. Not Rosa de . . ." Sam began.

"Rose was her stable name, but I wonder if she'd remember it." Jen paused and tapped her index finger against lips that were becoming chapped from the high desert wind. "Mom and Dad used to joke that they'd owned Rose for such a short time, she still spoke Spanish."

When Jen mentioned her parents, her face turned from thoughtful to worried.

Jed and Lila Kenworthy were quarreling. According to Jen, their fights had been going on for close to a year. Most were about staying on the ranch or moving to town.

Jen feared they were on the brink of a divorce.

"At least they had good memories of her," Sam put in, though she knew it was a lame thing to say.

Jen shook her head. "Not really. Dad says Rose was his last hope, and when he woke up one morning to find her gone, he just lost heart. A week later he started looking for a buyer for the Diamond K."

What could she say to help Jen? Sam bit her lower lip.

"While you and your mom were gone, these last few days, didn't your dad have a chance to rethink moving?"

"We thought it would help, having the house to himself," Jen said. "But all these things that are worrying him—" Jen threw up her hands in frustration. "They're real problems, but they're not our problems, you know what I mean? He's worried about money. Okay, I get that, but do you know why? Because he thinks I want cooler clothes."

Sam knew her astonishment must have shown, because Jen was nodding in agreement with her expression.

"Yeah, clothes for me, when I love getting my stuff from thrift stores." Jen parted her jacket to look down at her outfit. "Where else could I find a hot-pink blouse to go with these cranberry-colored cords? And he thinks Mom wants a new computer. Mom doesn't care anything about computers. She'd rather have a new mop, and I'm not joking. But once, just once, she mentioned something about it being slow logging on, when she was ordering a library book to be brought out on the bookmobile."

"Haven't you told him—"

"Oh, we've told him," Jen said. "And now his latest thing, last night, when we got home, isn't for me and Mom. He's been reading that weird little newspaper they hand out at the feed store, and he says everyone's trying to take advantage of the West anyway, so he might as well go to the city. The article that got him going was about European horse meat dealers coming to Nevada secretly, to buy wild horses."

"What?" Sam felt chills like icy rain down her spine. "It's not true, is it?"

"Of course not," Jen said.

Sam realized she'd closed her eyes against the nightmare images rushing into her mind. She opened her eyes wide. She could think about that later. Right now, she had to act like a best friend and help Jen.

"But Golden Rose could change everything, right?" Sam wanted to bite her tongue. False hope wasn't the kind of help Jen needed. But it was too late to take her words back.

"It *could* help! It really could!" Jen leaped up and hugged Sam's neck.

Jen jumped with joy, as far as her heavy coat allowed.

Sam smiled. She really hoped everything worked

out. But what if Jen pinned all her hopes on this horse and it wasn't Golden Rose?

"You promise you won't tell anyone," Jen said, as they remounted and left the canyon.

"If you didn't believe me when I swore the first time, why should you believe me the tenth?" Sam asked, but Jen was too lost in daydreams to answer.

While Sam took notes on the ghost town of Nugget, Jen kept staring at the ravine.

"I don't want anyone to know, except you, until I can catch her," Jen blurted.

"Hope you can rope better than I can, because—"

"Rope her? And traumatize her completely?" Jen gasped. "I'm not taking a chance on that. She'll just get used to me, and when she does, I'll show her to my dad."

*And we'll all live happily every after*, Jen's voice implied.

"You sound pretty sure that will end his plan to move," Sam said.

"I am sure," Jen snapped. "And I don't know why you're calling it a *plan*. It's more of a crazy idea. Don't you want me to stay?"

"Jen, you're my best friend in the world," Sam said. She swallowed hard and tried to keep her voice relaxed, but each time she thought of Jen moving, tears pricked at the corners of her eyes. "I hated it when you were gone for a few days. What do you think would happen to me if you actually moved?"

Jen gave a lopsided smile. "I think you'd be hanging around with Rachel and Daisy inside a week."

Rachel was Linc Slocum's beautiful, stuck-up daughter and Daisy was her pretty but airheaded friend.

"Oh, right. There's as much chance of that as—" Sam broke off. She'd just seen something almost as unlikely. "Tell me that's another mirage and I'll believe you."

Jen followed Sam's gaze across the range.

A sleek brown Thoroughbred came toward them at a gentle trot.

His rider rose in short stirrups. Posting.

"Who, around here, rides English?" Jen asked.

"Don't you recognize the horse?" Sam asked.

The animal's chocolate-colored neck and front legs gleamed in the winter sun. His body lined out like that of a greyhound.

"Oh my gosh," Jen murmured. "It's Sky and Ryan."

Ryan Slocum was Rachel's brother. He'd lived with their mother in Nottingham, England, until about two months ago. Sky Ranger was a Thoroughbred that Linc Slocum used for endurance work. Like chasing mustangs.

The first time Sam had seen the gelding, Linc had been using him to pursue the Phantom.

"You both live on the same ranch and you didn't know he rode English?" Sam asked. She looked over at Jen in time to see her friend push her glasses firmly up on her nose.

"Since he's been home, I've seen him around the horses," Jen said, lifting one shoulder. "But I haven't seen him ride."

"He's coming this way," Sam said.

Ryan didn't wear fancy jodhpurs, and Sam was glad. Her first impressions of the guy had been positive, and she wouldn't like it if people made fun of him. Around here, English riding gear would guarantee it.

Not that Jen looked like *she'd* mock him. She took in Ryan's jeans, glossy brown boots, and the open-necked white shirt that showed above his burgundy sweater as if she were memorizing them.

Ryan lifted a hand. They returned his wave, but he was still too far off for conversation.

"Don't—" Jen began.

"I won't tell him you saw Golden Rose." Sam sighed in frustration.

"Well, good," Jen said as Silly and Ace neighed a greeting. "But I was going to say, don't give him a hard time about riding Sky."

Sam mulled that over. Why should she? Unless he was getting Sky in shape for something she wouldn't approve of.

"Hallo," Ryan said.

His British accent made Sam smile. She just couldn't help it.

He didn't look like the guys from Darton High and he didn't act like them. He wore his coffee-brown hair a little long and didn't try to hide his intelligence.

"Hi," Sam said. "Why are you riding Sky way out here? Training for something?"

Jen groaned and shot Sam a scolding look, but Ryan didn't seem to take offense.

"Not really," he said. "The horse is rarely ridden and needed some work. Why? Is there an event coming up?"

Sam shrugged.

"In any case, I've taken him on as a project. Him and that lovely little Appaloosa, Hotspot. I must say, I don't understand why my father isn't keen on keeping the foal. What could he possibly have against that beautiful mare?"

"I think it's more what he has against the stallion. The father," Jen said.

"Yes?" Ryan looked intrigued and his tone coaxed them to go on.

"Didn't he tell you?" Sam asked.

"Actually, no." Ryan looked embarrassed. Because his father wouldn't talk with him? Or maybe because he was altogether ashamed of having Linc Slocum for a father.

"Was it one of your wild mustangs?" Ryan guessed.

"Probably not," Sam said. "She was stolen right out of a Gold Dust Ranch pasture by a stallion who turned out to be an endurance champion named Diablo."

Ryan rubbed Sky's neck as if assuring him Diablo would be a weak opponent. He mulled over the information for so long, Jen shifted in her saddle and Sam studied Sky.

The gelding hadn't broken a sweat and wasn't breathing hard. If Ryan was training for something, his horse appeared to be in top form.

"My father can be rather eccentric," Ryan said, finally.

Although the urge to applaud Ryan's conclusion was strong, Sam didn't. Saying something critical about your father was one thing. Listening to someone else say he was a nutcase was something else again.

Sam stuck to a safe topic. "How far are you taking him?"

For the first time, Ryan looked uncomfortable, and Sam felt instantly suspicious. Slocums were not to be trusted, even cute ones with accents.

"Not far," he said. "Actually, I often let him go where he likes."

A flush colored Ryan's skin and Sam glanced at Jen to see if she'd noticed. Probably so. Jen wouldn't meet Sam's eyes, but she was blushing, too.

Once more, Ryan held up his hand, this time in farewell.

"What's he's hiding?" Sam asked as soon as he'd ridden out of earshot.

"Nothing," Jen said. "He's embarrassed that he lets the horse be the boss."

"Think so?" Sam asked. "That really didn't seem like a very good explanation."

Jen continued to stare after Ryan. Her lips wore a slight smile as if she were confused by her own thoughts.

"The way his hair sort of falls on his forehead, doesn't it just make you want to brush it back for him?"

If Jen had asked, *Don't you just have a craving to eat bugs?* it would have surprised her less.

Could you suffer mental whiplash? Sam wondered.

"You have a crush on him," she said in disbelief.

"Of course I don't. I just think it's cool he's taking an interest in Sky and Hotspot." Silence crept in between each of Jen's words. "Especially Hotspot." The harder she tried to sound sensible, the less she did. "She's a beautiful mare. . . . "

"Yeah," Sam teased. "So beautiful, she makes you want to brush her forelock back out of her eyes."

"Shut up," Jen said, in a level tone that sounded like a request.

Sam laughed, glad that Jen was finally acting like herself again.

"Whatever," Jen said, dismissing Ryan with a word.

The wind had stopped. The orange morning sun had turned into a flat white disk and cold clamped down.

Sam pulled her gloves out of her pocket and worked them on. Ace felt the cold, too, or he'd take advantage of her distraction to act up.

"Good boy," Sam praised him, but the gelding only swished his tail in annoyance. If she could read his mind, Sam was pretty sure she'd see him thinking about the warm barn corral he shared with Sweetheart, Gram's old paint mare.

Keeping her reins in her left hand, she tugged the leather collar of her sheepskin-lined coat up to her chin. "I need to get home and strategize," Jen said.

Sam glanced at her friend. "Aren't you cold?"

Jen's nose was red. Her lips were a white that could turn blue any second, and yet her jacket hung open over her sweater.

"Not really. I'm thinking."

Sam knew she'd felt relieved too soon. Jen was so fixated on Golden Rose, she didn't even know she was cold.

But here came help. Or at least another distraction.

Crested head held high, a black horse surged toward them. She looked primitive and just barely under control, like a horse daubed in paint on an elk-skin tent. Her rider lacked a spear and shield, but his hair was ink black like the horse and he rode as if the two were one.

Yep, from a distance Jake Ely looked great, but Sam could tell from the set of his jaw that he was irritated.

Add Jen's presence to his irritation, and it was like pouring gasoline on a fire. The two never got along.

"Oh, make him disappear," Jen moaned as Jake rode closer. "I've got to meditate. If I can only go home, stretch out on my bed with a notebook, and lay out a plan, I can keep Dad from quitting his job and moving to the city. I'm just not up for a fight with Jake Ely right now."

## Chapter Four

Witch, Jake's black Quarter horse, liked to bully other horses. Ace had learned to stay out of reach, but Silly stretched her muzzle out in welcome, trying to be friends.

Witch was still five or six horse lengths away when her hindquarters tensed. Her trot turned jerky and her ears flattened to her skull. Her eyes flashed rivalry and her hooves jabbed the dirt as she approached.

A stranger to horses might not have noticed Witch's foul attitude, but Sam and Jen did. Only Jake's skillful riding kept Witch from wheeling to kick Silly.

With a whinny high-pitched as a foal's, Silly extended her head toward Ace, asking for help, but Jen acted first.

"What's that brainless beast you ride got against other horses?" she shouted.

Sam sighed. This whole day was going to be an emotional roller-coaster, apparently.

Jake kept his mare in check and ignored Jen's question.

"Morning." His greeting sounded like a reprimand. Sam and Jen knew Jake wasn't just stopping to shoot the breeze when he lifted his chin slightly and asked, "What's he doing out here?"

He had to be talking about Ryan Slocum. Even though he'd ridden out of sight, his tracks remained. Jake had probably picked up Sky's hoofprints at the Gold Dust Ranch, but how could he know who was riding him?

Jake stared toward Lost Canyon. His coat was open over a faded blue shirt and his Shoshone hair was pulled back under his black Stetson. Sam couldn't see Jake's eyes, but his casual posture said he was indifferent to the answer. Still, the fact that he didn't ride on after saying hi proved he was faking.

"*He* who?" Jen taunted. Then, when Jake didn't take the bait, she added, "Last time I looked, this was open range. I suppose just about anyone can ride out here."

Jake's hat brim dipped a fraction of an inch. "Rustlers, butchers, con men," he muttered in agreement.

"Your jealousy is showing," Jen said.

"Oh, yeah. I like the sissy look of a man who can't sit down on his horse for fear it's not tough enough to carry him."

"Stop it," Sam said. "I've heard you admit that some of the best riders in the world use English saddles."

Jake kept quiet, but she could feel his irritation. So now he thought she'd betrayed him. Too bad. Jake and Jen always put her in the middle. At least she didn't mention the black-and-white poster of Mexican cavalrymen riding down hillsides that Jake had shown her once. It was from some 1950s movie and the saddles were smaller and lighter than Western saddles. They'd looked a lot like English saddles. And, if she remembered right, Jake had said something like, "That's ridin'."

"If you're referring to Ryan Slocum," Jen said, "he's giving Sky, their endurance horse, some exercise."

Again, Jake gave a small nod.

Seeing that she couldn't bait him into further argument, Jen gathered her reins and backed Silly away from the other two.

"Fun as this has been, I'd better be on my way," Jen said to Sam. She backhanded one white-blond braid over her shoulder. "Mom was still in her bathrobe when I left and she was already asking if I'd unpacked my suitcase. And I have a few other plans to get in order before it's time to start thinking about school."

Jen widened her eyes meaningfully toward Sam.

Sam tried to cover for Jen's not-so-subtle hint.

"I think this project is going to be fun. I'll go over our field notes and start typing them up. I don't have anything to do for the rest of vacation. Unless you want to come back tomorrow?"

"Oh, yeah!" Jen raised her hand in a fist and pumped it skyward, then sent Silly loping for home.

*Oh, nice, Jen.* Sam stirred her legs against the saddle leathers and let Ace start for home. Good thing Jen was aiming at a career in veterinary medicine and not espionage.

"What's she up to?" Jake said, as Witch fell into step beside Ace.

"As if I'd tell you."

"Something to do with Slocum or with that ghost town?"

"Hey, I need to ask you something," Sam said suddenly.

"Nice diversion. Real pro, but answer me first."

"I can't. I promised I wouldn't."

Jake sighed, then gave a shrug that said he took promises seriously, but couldn't see how anything Jen said warranted such a vow.

"The Kenworthys sold their ranch to Slocum not long after I had to go to San Francisco, right?"

Jake's shoulders tensed. He'd finally tried to duck guilt when it came at him, but he still felt responsible for the riding accident that had sent Sam to the hospital, and then to San Francisco for two years.

"Around then," he said.

"So why don't they have a lot of money?"

Hundreds of acres of ranchland, complete with

water rights and outbuildings, had to be worth a lot. Maybe Jed had made a bad decision and wasted the money quickly. Maybe that's why he felt guilty that Jen and her mother didn't have nice things.

"Back taxes," Jake said. "Plus other debt. In that drought he lost cattle. Like everyone else, he sold some for less than he'd paid for them, but that didn't take into account raising 'em, feeding 'em, trucking them to market."

Sam felt a surge of thankfulness. Her family had been so lucky not to lose River Bend.

"Not that it's any of your business, Brat."

"It is if Jen's dad makes them move," Sam said.

"Thought that was just a rumor."

"I hope so."

Slowly, as if he was fighting the pull of his own curiosity, Jake looked back toward Lost Canyon.

Let him look, Sam thought. He was jealous of Ryan and she didn't blame him. Besides, if he was fretting over Ryan, he wouldn't see her searching the Calico Mountains, hoping and fearing she'd see the Phantom.

All at once, her imagination bloomed with a thought darker than a nightmare.

"You said butchers," she blurted. "What were you talking about?"

"Nothing in particular."

"Jake, do you know anything about . . ." Sam told herself not to be stupid. Saying it wouldn't make it true, but the words stuck in her throat.

"About what?" Jake tilted his head back slightly so he could study her without the barrier of his hat brim. "Simmer down, Brat. Do I know anything about what?"

"Horsemeat dealers."

"I know it's illegal to sell wild horses, or stolen horses to 'em."

"But are there any around here?"

"You've been out to the Mineral auction yards with Brynna, right? When you were looking for the rustlers who had mustangs?"

"No. I recognized the truck before we got out there," Sam said.

She'd actually been glad to miss seeing the auction yards.

Sam didn't know why she couldn't—no matter how hard she tried—treat animals like lesser creatures. She didn't think of them as pets, really, but she couldn't help trying to understand what they were thinking. Maybe she'd spent too much time away from ranch life. Or maybe she'd inherited a soft heart from her city-bred mother.

"But, are you saying people take horses out there and sell them for—"

"Well, some folks don't ask. But if you could see the stock that gets trucked in . . ." Jake sighed. "Scarred animals, lame ones, unbreakable crazy ones, and some that are just too old for work. . . ." Jake's voice trailed off, then came back softer than usual. "Those old ponies aren't going to a retirement home, Samantha."

"That's awful," Sam protested.

Ace jumped sideways, startled by her shout and the tension in her legs.

"Well, Jim McDonald, the brand inspector, keeps people from catching wild ones and selling 'em like they did in the old days. So don't get into a tizzy about that."

*A tizzy.* The words were so condescending, they made Sam mad. Mad enough not to talk for the rest of the ride.

When the River Bend bridge came into view, she expected Jake to ride on home, toward Three Ponies Ranch, but he turned Witch toward the bridge.

"What are you doing?" Sam asked, finally breaking her vow of silence.

"Ain't you ever heard of Western hospitality?" Jake drawled.

"Don't talk like . . ." Sam closed her lips. He'd done it on purpose to irritate her. Jake had such stupid guy ways of trying to snap her out of sadness.

As two sets of hooves clopped across the wooden planks, though, she had to ask.

"Why are you following me?"

"Just reporting for work, ma'am," Jake said.

"There are no colts to break. Dad's home. And Pepper and Ross are back from Idaho, so I don't think Dallas needs you."

"I'm insulted," Jake said, but the half smile on his lips said he wasn't anything of the kind. "You've overlooked the fact that I've got more than muscle power going for me. Got me a brain, too." Jake tapped his temple with the index finger of his free hand.

Sam couldn't imagine what he was talking about. Dad, Brynna, and Gram could handle anything Jake could. Except tracking, maybe, but she had the feeling he was talking about something else.

Jake obviously wanted her to beg for details.

Forget it. Out of habit, Sam tightened her reins, but she didn't have to. Ace had already stopped at the hitching post where she tied him to unsaddle and brush him before putting him back in the barn.

Jake sat lazy in the saddle, watching her.

Sam's patience lasted until she'd stripped off Ace's saddle and draped the blanket over it to air.

"Okay, why do you think we need your pea-sized brain?"

Jake laughed. "They don't, but you do." Jake swept off his Stetson and made a bow. "Meet your new math tutor."

*"What?"*

The Rhode Island Red hens squawked and fluttered, disturbed in their search for slow winter bugs by Sam's screech. Blaze, the ever-watchful ranch dog, came trotting from the barn.

Jake dismounted, ground-tied Witch, and rubbed his palms together like a soap opera villain. "You're going to eat, sleep, and breathe algebra for the rest of vacation."

This could not be true.

"Dad!" Sam ran toward the barn, yelling.

Algebra on school days was bad enough.

Before she reached the barn, Dallas, River Bend's foreman, stepped into the doorway and pointed toward the house.

Sam swung around to run the other way. Jake was still laughing, watching her run around like one of those silly hens. She'd almost reached the house when the screen door opened and Dad stepped out onto the wooden porch.

A spicy aroma of chilies and eggs wafted from the house. Gram must be practicing what she'd learned during her vacation at a New Mexico cooking school. Sam's stomach growled in anticipation, but food didn't matter. Nothing mattered except her last few days of freedom.

"Dad," Sam said, trying to catch her breath. "Jake says he's my new math tutor."

Dad drank from his steaming cup of coffee. He held it up longer than a sip warranted. He gazed over the rim and his eyes settled on Jake.

Once he'd swallowed, he asked, "When are you kids gonna outgrow teasing and tormenting each other?"

"Maybe never," Sam said. "So he's not telling the truth?"

"Well, yeah, he is."

Sam put her hands on her hips in fury, then let them slide off. Never once had she won an argument with Dad by yelling. They were both too stubborn.

"Okay, I know I'm not doing that well in algebra. But *you* can help me. Or—Jen! Jen's really good at math. She's in the same classes as Jake and she's only a freshman."

"We thought you'd get more studyin' done if you worked with Jake."

Sam took a deep breath. That battle was lost. She tried to save her vacation.

"But not *now*, right? Not during vacation."

Dad shifted his weight to one leg. He glanced toward the kitchen door behind him, as if he expected backup from someone inside.

Wait. *We thought you'd get more studyin' done . . .*

*We* thought?

This was so simple, she should have figured it out at once. Her father wouldn't do this to her. And even serious, school-is-your-highest-priority Gram had never suggested she ruin a vacation with algebra.

Neither Dad nor Gram would do it.

But Sam knew who would.

## Chapter Five

The door opened behind Dad.

Brynna stepped out, pulling a black fleecy coat on over the khaki uniform that made her look like what she was: the director of the Bureau of Land Mangement's Willow Springs Wild Horse corrals, the woman who'd backed down Linc Slocum and other bad guys, the one who'd helped save the Phantom twice.

She didn't look like a traitor.

Maybe that was a traitor's secret. First, she fooled you into thinking she was on your side.

"I'll probably be late," Brynna said, flipping her red French braid out of her coat collar. "I'm getting a late start, and there'll be lots of things left undone while we were gone."

Brynna perched on her tiptoes to give Dad's cheek a kiss.

Dad's free arm hugged her to him, but he nodded

toward Sam as if Brynna needed a reminder that they weren't alone.

Sam swallowed hard when Brynna turned toward her, grinning.

"Good morning," she chirped.

Sam didn't know what to say, so she glanced meaningfully at her watch. It was almost noon. Not that she cared if Brynna was late for work.

"Hi," Sam managed, but she heard her own voice and knew she'd addressed Brynna with the same enthusiasm she'd use for a rattlesnake she found curled up in her boot.

"What's up?" Brynna asked. Her voice was casual, but a frown line appeared between her blue eyes.

When Sam didn't answer, Brynna glanced at Dad.

"Algebra," Dad said.

"Oh, right." Brynna sighed, looking relieved. She jingled the car keys in her coat pocket and crossed the porch. She leaned toward Sam as if she'd give her a peck on the cheek, too.

Sam glanced toward Jake. One hand rubbed the back of his neck as it did when he was uncomfortable. Jake hated scenes. Sam was pretty sure he'd thought everything was settled, or he wouldn't have shown up.

By looking away, Sam had dodged Brynna's kiss. She couldn't really say if she'd done it on purpose, but Brynna stood close enough that Sam saw her disappointment.

Well, what did Brynna expect? To just march in here and start changing things?

Sam felt justified and guilty at the same time. This stepmother thing wasn't going to be as easy as she'd thought.

Once more, Brynna's keys jingled.

"I'll take care of it," Dad said.

*It?* Now she was an *it?* Sam clenched her fists so tightly, she felt her fingernails against her palms.

"Thanks," Brynna answered, then blew Dad a kiss.

Another kiss. How many did that make? Like, a dozen before she even got off the porch?

Brynna didn't make another move to touch Sam, but she gave Ace a quick pat as she went striding toward the white BLM truck parked between Dad's truck and Gram's old yellow Buick.

Sam crossed her arms and looked up at Dad. Slowly, he came down the porch steps until they were nearly eye-to-eye.

"On the morning of the wedding, I stopped in town," Dad began, and Sam knew this was going to be bad if it had been brewing that long. "I stopped by the post office and there was a notice from the school saying you were failing algebra."

"They send those out to everybody," Sam protested.

Dad splashed the last bit of his coffee on the dirt that would be a flowerbed, come spring. Then he gave Sam a skeptical look.

"Okay, not everybody," Sam amended. "But it doesn't mean I'm failing for sure."

"Good, because this is high school you're in now. If you fail at the semester, you'll lose your credit. That means you'll repeat algebra in summer school. And that's *all* you'll be doing, Samantha."

Sam could actually feel the embarrassment. Her face flushed hot as if she'd opened an oven door. Dad was telling her she wouldn't be working with cattle or horses or even with the HARP girls this summer, if she didn't pull up her grade.

"But I can improve before the end of the semester. After we go back to school, I've still got two weeks," Sam told him.

"We're going to make it two and a half." Dad brushed his hands together, then hung a thumb in one of his back pockets. "Every morning, before you go riding, you'll spend two hours working on algebra. That doesn't mean you skip your regular chores, either."

"Two hours?" Sam gasped.

"At least two hours. Jake is here to go over whatever graded work you've got stashed in your backpack. He'll do sort of a diagnosis and tell me if it should be more."

"But Dad—"

"That's it," Dad said. "Go have yourself something to eat. Your gram's apparently not gonna quit cooking until next Christmas, so help her out. Then get to work. After that, come on down to the barn. And wear your oldest sneakers. No boots for the chore I have in mind."

Sam stared after Dad as he walked toward the barn. This ruined everything. How could she use the rest of vacation to save Jen from moving, if she was confined to the kitchen table with an algebra book?

Shaking her head in disbelief, Sam turned to Jake.

To his credit, Jake looked embarrassed for her.

He removed his hat and fanned himself with it, although the temperature was probably near freezing.

"C'mon Brat," he said, and together they went indoors.

The kitchen smelled like pumpkin pie.

Gram turned from the stove so fast her denim skirt swirled and her gray hair, twisted and held up with a clip, threatened to break loose.

"Can I interest you two in some dessert, completely unencumbered by a meal?" Gram asked.

She didn't wait for a response before pulling little pastry turnovers off a cookie sheet. She shook her fingers from the heat and put a plate of four on the kitchen table.

"These are pumpkin *empanadas*. They can cool while you run up and get your backpack," Gram said.

"For your second dessert course, I'm making *sopa-pillas*."

She sounded too darn happy, Sam thought.

"This is a plot," she muttered. "You're all in on it, aren't you?"

"Of course, dear," Gram said.

Algebra went down better with a plate of dessert, Sam decided, later.

Together, she and Jake had finished off a platter of *sopapillas*, little pillows of fried dough drizzled with honey.

They'd eaten so many, Sam felt a little queasy, but they'd certainly sweetened Jake's mood. By the time he'd finished sorting through her graded algebra papers, Jake told her that she wasn't doomed to failure.

"I don't think you're that bad at it," Jake said, tapping an "F" paper with a sticky index finger. "But I bet you're not paying attention."

"It's so boring," Sam moaned, but Jake's face said he wasn't sympathetic. "So what are you going to tell Dad?"

"Two hours should be enough."

Sam rocked in her chair. This wasn't the best news Jake could have given her. Or the worst.

She could keep her mind on algebra two hours a day. She stared at the clock on the whitewashed kitchen wall. If she got up at her normal time and got all her chores done early, two hours would mean it was only about ten o'clock.

The ride to Nugget wouldn't take more than an hour. She and Jen could work together on their project at the same time they tried to catch Golden Rose.

Jake was asking her something about an integer, but the ticking of the kitchen clock reminded Sam of hooves. Careful hooves. A watchful horse . . .

"How could we tell if someone was stalking the Phantom's herd for horsemeat?"

Jake pushed back his chair. "That's what's getting you in trouble. Not concentrating. Do this," Jake said, tapping a list he'd made for her. "And I'll check it day after tomorrow. Now, I'm out of here."

"Is he paying you for this?" Sam said, following Jake to the door.

He flashed her a white smile as he lifted his black Stetson from a front porch hook, but he didn't answer.

"To come make fun of me and eat Gram's cooking?"

"You bet," Jake said.

As the door closed behind him, Sam remembered one of Linc Slocum's dopey Western sayings. It suited Jake perfectly.

He looked as happy as a dog with two tails to wag.

✳ ✳ ✳

"You're going to be jogging the pasture," Dad told Sam when she arrived in the barn. "In weather like this, the horses get lazy. I want you to go out and jog outside the fence line of the ten-acre pasture and get them stirred up."

"From outside, I can't exactly chase them," Sam said.

"You won't have to," Dad said. "They'll chase you. It's the herd instinct."

"Are you sure?" Sam asked.

"Never seen it fail," Dad said. "'Course, there's other work to be done."

Dad glanced toward the feed room. There was an awful closet in there, full of everything that wouldn't fit elsewhere. They called it Blackbeard's Closet. She guessed it was named for Blackbeard the pirate, because *Blue*beard's closet was in a legend about some guy who kept the bodies of his curious wives in his closet.

So, Blackbeard's closet was better, but for months, Dad had been threatening her with "straightening" it.

"Oh no," Sam said. Holding her hands up like a shield, she started backing toward the barn door.

"Make sure Buff gets a good workout," Dad said. "He's carryin' a little extra girth he could do without and I don't think I'm gonna get to him today."

"Okay," Sam said.

Buffalo was a dark-brown River Bend gelding

who'd been in town for the summer. About twelve years old, with thick hair and the temperament of a pet, he could herd cattle and baby-sit young riders. When a friend of Gram's asked if River Bend would rent her a horse for her grandchildren's summer visit, Dad had trailered Buff into town and asked only that they keep him healthy and well fed in exchange.

Sam sprinted toward the corral before Dad could give her something else to do, and five minutes later, she'd decided this was her favorite chore on the ranch.

The ground was dry, covered with sparse grass. Though the air was still cold, dusk hadn't settled in yet and the sky was bright.

There were eight horses in the ten-acre pasture right now, six saddle horses and two mustangs-in-training for the Horse and Rider Assistance Program. Ace and Sweetheart brought the count of the home herd to ten horses, and Sam had no doubt they'd be jealous as soon as the other horses began running.

Dark Sunshine and Popcorn, the two mustangs, marked her arrival before any of the other horses. The buckskin mare and albino gelding stood shoulder to shoulder, with their heads held high and ears pricked to catch Sam's sounds. If this scheme of Dad's really worked, she'd bet the mustangs would be first to join her herd.

Sam jiggled the gate to get all the horses' attention and Buff took notice of her, too. He trotted a few steps closer and gave a low nicker.

"No treats for you, boy," Sam said, and the brown gelding swished his tail as if he were insulted.

She made sure the gate was closed and latched.

"Here goes," she said.

Sam started jogging.

All the horses were clustered at the far end of the pasture, but each head lifted at the sound of her running steps.

Who would be the first to join her?

Sam was amazed when the first horse to toss his head in excitement was Amigo.

The old sorrel was graying around his eyes and lips, but Dallas said he was still the best roping horse on the place. Sam wouldn't contradict him. Dallas had been riding Amigo the day he had to rope her and Ace and drag them from a flash flood sweeping down the La Charla River. Clearly, Amigo was now interested in having fun. With ears pricked forward and eyes fixed on Sam, he stared across the top fence rail and jogged beside her.

Nike fell in next. The blood bay had the lanky conformation of a running Quarter horse. Pepper, the young cowboy from Idaho, loved riding him. Within seconds, Strawberry, Tank, and Buff added themselves to the herd.

Amigo had fallen back with the others by the time Sam had made a full circuit of the pasture.

Jeepers-Creepers, the rat-tailed Appaloosa that

Brynna had been riding lately, decided the gathering was safe, and became a part of it.

It was really working. Sam kept a steady pace as she listened to the horses cavorting alongside and behind her. To them, it was a game, and she felt lucky to be part of it. She thought of the lonely, foggy afternoons she'd sat at the bay window in Aunt Sue's San Francisco flat, pining for the ranch and its horses. She was back now and she loved it. She offered a silent thanks that she had returned.

Hot breath on her neck made Sam run faster. She glanced over her shoulder and saw Buff had taken the lead. His trot extended to catch her and he bumped into the fence in his excitement. When his head tipped to one side, he looked like he was smiling.

"Fall back a little, can't you?" she huffed. "Or pass me?"

But Buff stayed right behind her, sniffing for sugar cubes.

A chorus of sudden neighs came from the mustangs. Dark Sunshine and Popcorn shook their heavy manes and launched into the band.

It was perfect, simply perfect. Her fantasy of running with the Phantom's band was almost coming true. He wasn't here, inside the fences of the ranch where he'd been born. And she hoped he never was, but she could pretend.

Wind combed her auburn hair back from her face. Blue-gray sky and fence rails and faraway mountains smeared into a dizzy circle around them. She smelled crushed grass, cold dirt, and horses. The muscles in her thighs stretched and bunched and stretched again.

All around, nickers and snorts mingled with the thud of hooves.

It had been a long time since she'd played horses with girlfriends on the elementary school playground, and it had never been like this.

Today, the land of make-believe was a wonderful place to be, and Sam never wanted to leave.

# *Chapter Six*

When Sam's lungs began to burn and her legs turned wobbly, she slowed, and the horses began drifting away.

She leaned against the corral gate, watching them go. Amigo and Strawberry returned to the far end of the pasture, Popcorn trailing a few steps behind them. Buff snorted and stamped a front hoof, and Sam wondered if he was thanking her for the workout.

Only Dark Sunshine lingered. She faced the house, pretending interest, while one ear swiveled to hear Sam catch her breath.

When Sam's breathing had returned to normal, the mare was still there.

"Hey, pretty girl," Sam called.

The buckskin swished her glossy black tail, gave a little buck, and then trotted off to join the others.

She's happy, Sam thought. Although the mare had been neglected by her first owner and abused by her second, she was settling in at River Bend.

Suddenly Sam knew it wasn't wishful thinking to imagine Dark Sunshine's foal with the Phantom might grow to be hers. Really hers.

Sam pressed her hands over her lips to keep from yipping in delight and scaring the young mare.

If only she could stroke Dark Sunshine and speak to the colt or filly inside her, it might be like it was with human babies. In a TV documentary, she'd seen newborn babies turning away from the voices of doctors and nurses to focus on the voices they knew—those of their parents.

Even if that day was far off, Dark Sunshine had trusted Sam enough to dawdle behind the other horses. That was progress.

Sam had latched the gate behind her and she was heading for the house when Dad's truck bumped over the bridge. A glimpse of red hair told her Pepper was driving. The young River Bend cowboy braked to a stop. Both he and Ross got out. Ross slammed the door and headed for the barn, while Pepper just stood there.

He wore a heavy gray coat over a couple of other layers of clothes. Sam knew he hated the cold, but she thought something more than that hampered his movements as he approached.

"Hey Sam," he said. His boots scuffed as if he

were dragging them to slow him down, and though his voice was cheerful, his mouth looked tight with worry. He watched the ground as he walked and his hat brim hid his eyes.

"Hey, Pepper," she replied.

He stopped and nodded for no apparent reason. "When's Brynna comin' home? Do you know?"

According to Sam's watch, it was already three o'clock, but Brynna had left late. Besides, she didn't know Brynna's working hours yet.

"I don't," she said. "It's her first day back at Willow Springs, and she thought there might be a lot of work stacked up."

Sam couldn't imagine there was something Brynna could handle and Dad couldn't.

Unless it was about mustangs.

Sam had to ask. "Is it something to do with wild horses?"

Pepper exhaled. He sounded like a weary old man.

"Well, yeah," he said. "Don't take this to heart, but I found a dead one."

Sam's head spun.

*Not the Phantom, please don't let it be him*. But then she thought of Moon, the Phantom's night-black son. And a pair of blood bays that had run with the herd since the beginning of last summer, too. She'd grieve for any dead horse.

"Do you think we should call Brynna or wait for her?" Pepper asked.

Sam couldn't focus on Brynna until she knew more.

"Which one is it?" Sam managed.

On purpose, she called the horse it, not him. And Pepper hadn't spoken, so maybe the horse was unfamiliar.

Maybe it wasn't a mustang at all. Suddenly irritated by Pepper's cowboy habit of deliberating before he spoke, she demanded, "What does it look like?"

"It's not the Phantom. That's for sure. Or that young black you took a fancy to."

A sigh of relief rocked Sam.

"It's a paint mare, red-brown spotted," Pepper said. He made a wide gesture over one side of his chest, showing how the horse was marked. "A young horse, probably has—uh, had, some draft blood."

The description sounded familiar, but it wasn't one of the pintos belonging to Mrs. Allen, the lady who owned the Blind Faith Mustang Sanctuary. Neither Calico nor Ginger could be mistaken for young animals.

"Died between here and Three Ponies Ranch. Jake found her, saw me and Ross comin' by, and flagged us down. Thought Brynna should be told."

That almost guaranteed the horse was a mustang. Jake had a phenomenal memory and a great eye for detail. If the horse had belonged to a neighboring ranch, he would have recognized it. And he was right, since Brynna worked for the Bureau of Land

Management, the government agency charged with keeping an eye on all wild horses, she should be notified.

"He thinks she died of something bad," Pepper added. "Illness or something."

Sam was so startled, her shoulders jerked.

Illness? When Linc Slocum hatched a plan to build a resort, a super dude ranch, he'd tried to create a Western mood by putting out hay along the highway, baiting wild horses so that out-of-town investors would admire them.

Even though he'd been arrested and punished for the illegal activity, Sam had assumed a mustang had come along looking for hay, and been struck by a car. Horses didn't always look both ways before crossing a street. Especially wild horses.

The thought of illness, on the other hand, made chills race down Sam's arms. Because they lived in close communities, disease was always a threat to mustangs.

Suddenly, she remembered the horse Pepper had described.

"I hope I'm wrong," Sam said. "But last week, when I saw the Phantom's herd, he had a new lead mare. A red-brown paint." Sam swallowed hard. She didn't want to ask the next question. "Did this horse have a flaxen mane and tail?"

Pepper stood quietly, but not from uncertainty. He frowned and kicked his boot toe in the dirt.

He nodded. "Yep."

So the mare had been with the Phantom's band, just days ago.

If it was something contagious . . . if it was deadly . . . Sam's mind swam with awful possibilities. Not only could disease wipe out Phantom's herd, it could infect domestic horses who'd been around them. Ace. Witch. Chocolate Chip, Quinn Ely's gelding. Queen, the red dun who'd once been the Phantom's lead mare.

Sam was so involved with thinking of domestic horses that might be in danger, she didn't notice Dad until he stood beside her.

"What kinda nightmares are you giving yourself now?" he asked.

Sam shook her head. Why should she pile her misgivings on Dad? He had little affection for the wild horses who competed with the cattle for grass. After all, cattle supported the River Bend Ranch.

"You're afraid this is one of the Phantom's band. Am I right?" He paused until Sam nodded. "We won't bury the mare until Brynna takes a look, but I'm gonna drive out and make sure she wasn't killed by that cougar. Do you want to ride out there with me?"

It was a gruesome offer, but Sam appreciated it. Dad must have stopped thinking of her as a little kid.

Of course she didn't *want* to go. She didn't want to see any dead horse, but she had to know if a disease could be spreading through the Phantom's herd.

"I'll go," Sam said. "I think I should."

❀ ❀ ❀

Sam had no appetite for dinner that night. Her mind couldn't erase the image of the big paint mare, who'd been fierce and bossy just days ago, now dead.

"Sorry, Gram," she said. "The chicken looks good and it smells incredible, but I don't seem to be hungry."

Dad and Brynna were doing a better job of appreciating Gram's spicy Southwestern dinner.

"I'll have Sam's share," Dad said.

Then Brynna chimed in. "This is wonderful, Grace. Whoever thought of combining chili peppers and chocolate was a genius. What did you say this sauce is called again?"

"*Mole*," Gram said. "Like olé, but you add an *m* on the front."

Good manners won out over emotions when you were an adult, Sam supposed. Although none of them discussed the dead horse at the dinner table, Sam knew they were all thinking about her.

Dr. Scott had met Brynna, Dad, Sam, and Jake at the scene of the mare's death. He said he was unable to state a cause of death without further study.

They'd have to wait to learn if Phantom and his band had been exposed to danger.

They finished the meal in silence, but no one left the table.

"How did the study session with Jake go?" Brynna asked, finally.

"Fine," Sam said, looking down at her plate. "I'm

not as hopeless as he thought I'd be."

"Good," Brynna said. "And how's your room?"

"My room?" Sam made a mental tour of her bedroom. "It's the same as always."

"Hmm," Brynna's tone was puzzled. "I thought that since you're on vacation, you might have a little time to clean up your room."

*Va-ca-tion.* Mentally, Sam sounded the word out and defined it for Brynna. Days off weren't meant for dusting and folding and picking up.

"Maybe I'll come up tonight after dinner and give you some suggestions," Brynna offered.

"Uh, no. That's okay," Sam said.

"Well then . . ." Brynna's voice trailed off. She leaned back in her chair, surveyed the kitchen, then perked up. "Since Sam wants to clean her room alone after dinner—"

"Wait," Sam said. "I didn't say—"

"—I'll help you clean the kitchen, Grace. How would that be?"

To judge by her expression, Gram was no more thrilled by Brynna's offer of help than Sam had been, but she was more polite.

"There's not much to do, dear," Gram said. Then she shot a quick glance at Dad and turned back to Brynna with a smile. "But thank you. I'd love some company."

"Great," Brynna said. "I'll just go upstairs and change out of my uniform. I'll be right back."

As Brynna sprinted up the stairs, Dad spread his hands wide. His sheepish smile included Sam and Gram.

"I think she's just figuring out where she fits in," he said.

"That's to be expected," Gram said.

After Gram was so generous, Sam couldn't very well complain. Still, math and room cleaning were two things she hated. Brynna had insisted she review math every day and now she had to clean her room, too.

Sam tried to be understanding. Her life at River Bend hadn't changed that much. It was still home. Brynna, on the other hand, had left a cozy apartment, where she could do whatever she wanted, any time of the day or night. Now, she was surrounded by people and she had to consider what they thought and wanted every minute she was home.

Sam crossed her arms and cinched them tight against her body. She'd be nice, but she was drawing the line now. Extra algebra and after-dinner housework were the limit. The best she could do was keep quiet. She would, but only because Brynna loved mustangs.

An hour later, Sam had dusted the shelves that held her collection of glass horses. That didn't take long, but arranging the horses into little herds and family groups did. Next, she made her bed so that all of the blankets were on top of the mattress instead of draped across the floor. After that, she stacked her horse magazines inside a big plastic box that Gram had bought to fit under her bed.

Now, Sam stood with her hands on her hips, wondering what else would fit in that box and slide out of sight. Stray socks didn't seem like a good choice, but they were the only things she could see that would fit.

The telephone's ring sounded downstairs in the kitchen. When Gram called up that it was Jen, Sam felt rescued. Besides, Jen was probably the only one who'd understand how she felt about the mare's death.

She was also relieved to see that Gram, Dad, and Brynna were in the living room, watching a special on television. That meant she'd have some privacy while she talked with Jen.

"Hi," she began. "I'm so scared for the Phantom! One of the mares that's been running with his herd was found dead. She might have had a contagious disease—"

Jen didn't gasp. She didn't ask why. She didn't even seem to hear.

"I got my parents talking about Golden Rose," Jen said. Her voice was quiet, almost a whisper, so Sam guessed Jed and Lila were nearby. "It was actually the most the two of them have talked together for weeks."

"That's great," Sam said. Her news could wait,

she guessed, but Jen shouldn't have just ignored it.

"Yeah, they said one of the things that made her unusual was a 'double mane factor' in her breeding. She was supposed to have a big bushy mane and a full tail. Lots fuller than most light-colored horses, 'cause, you know, a lot of them have sort of wispy-thin manes and tails."

"Cool," Sam said. And it was, but didn't Jen care about the Phantom?

"You know how Sundance is a sort of orange-gold palomino? Mom and Dad planned to breed a fancy style of palomino they'd call Fire and Ice. Get it? The body would be flame colored and the mane silvery white like ice."

"That sounds great. I bet it would have attracted a lot of people. And with that double-mane factor—"

"Right. But I didn't tell them I've found her, not yet. What I want to do is catch her and just lead her in. Surprise them, you know?"

"Did you get any hints on how to tell if it's really her? I mean, it probably is, because we would have heard if anyone else was missing a horse—"

"Not just any horse—"

"But she could be a mustang."

"You must be joking." Jen's tone was scornful. "Did you see her conformation? Remember, we're talking about centuries of careful matches, not random crossbreeding like horses on the range. And when she peered around the corner of that building at us? She looked really smart."

Sam realized her fingers had curled tighter and tighter around the telephone receiver. Not only had Jen ignored Sam's awful news, she'd just insulted the conformation, good looks, and intelligence of wild horses.

"I hope she wasn't anywhere near the Phantom's herd," Sam said.

Though she was irritated with Jen, Sam really hoped not. It would be awful if Jen had found the mare, only to lose her to disease.

Jen still wasn't listening.

"You know, I've been thinking. I'll bring some sweet grain in my saddlebags tomorrow. While you're taking some more notes about Nugget—I think you should start with the general store, don't you?—I'll try to lure her close enough to touch."

So Jen played with the horse while Sam did the schoolwork? Sam pushed aside another twinge of irritation.

"Because if she has been with the Phantom's herd," Sam continued, "she might have been exposed—"

"And then, once I've gentled her enough to—" Jen broke off suddenly and her voice was scared. "What are you talking about?"

Now that Sam had Jen's full attention, she didn't really want to tell her.

"I'm talking about a dead horse that was found on

the range, Jen, just a few miles from Nugget."

Jen's silence made Sam feel awful, but neither of them could dodge the truth. Something had just killed one horse, and she might not be the last.

## Chapter Seven

"Jake found a dead mare on the range," Sam explained to Jen. "She was a big beautiful paint that I'd seen just last week for the first time. Jen, she didn't look at all sick then. Her coat was glossy. She was just prancing around. That's what worries me. A horse could be sick and you might not even know it."

"And they think it was disease," Jen's tone turned scientific. "What exactly?"

Dad called from the living room, "Time to go to bed, Sam."

"But it's vacation," Sam protested, then lowered her voice to keep talking to Jen. "They're not sure, but there were no marks on her."

"It could be congenital, then," Jen said thoughtfully. "Something she was born with. Like people, you know, who have a heart defect and except for that they're healthy."

Suddenly Dad was in the kitchen. "Vacation or not, it's time for you to skedaddle. You can talk with Jen tomorrow."

"Jen, I have to get off." Sam made her tone piti-ful. "And I can't go to Nugget tomorrow until I do *algebra—for two hours.*"

Sam noticed Dad didn't look the least bit apolo-getic. And he kept standing there.

"So," Sam continued, "I'll call you the instant I finish and we'll start out at the same time."

"I should leave right now," Jen fretted. "What if she was in contact with that mare and it's some con-dition that, with treatment—"

"Sam." Dad's voice was like a whiplash.

Sam turned away from him and cupped her hand over the space between the phone's mouthpiece and her lips.

"There's nothing you can do up there in the dark, idiot. It could be dangerous," Sam whispered. She sneaked a peek at her father's face. He wasn't furious yet, but he was getting there. "I'll call you first thing tomorrow."

"Now." Dad growled.

"Bye."

Sam woke up struggling with her sheets.

She was swathed in them, wrapped tightly as a mummy. What had she been dreaming? Something that made her feel imprisoned and scared.

But it was just a dream. She kicked at the sheets tangled around her ankles and finally wiggled free.

Okay. She was in her room.

It was still dark. She blinked at her bedside clock, brought the numbers into focus, and saw that it was only four o'clock. Downstairs, she heard the heater click on. It must be cold, because Dad didn't get up and turn it on until five-thirty.

*Go to sleep*, Sam told herself. Who but an idiot got up at four A.M. on the last Saturday of winter vacation? Not Sam Forster, that was for darn sure.

Sam closed her eyes again, but just for a minute.

In searing white light the clacking skeleton stallion that had chased her through her dreams suddenly reappeared on her closed eyelids. That nightmare image brought her fully awake. He wasn't just after her. He was after the Phantom.

Her horse needed her.

She had to go to his valley. That's what the dream was telling her. The Phantom and his herd were threatened by two dangers: the horsemeat dealers and disease.

Sam sat up, shivering. She kept the blankets draped around her as she pulled her legs up against her chest, and propped her chin on her knees.

What was that? She felt chills, as if she were being watched. She sensed, rather than heard, a repeated clack. But it wasn't bones. Not a skeleton horse. It was the sound of a hoof on the wooden bridge to River Bend Ranch.

Sam leaned close to her window, eyes straining through the night. From this angle, she couldn't see the entire bridge. The part she saw was empty.

The sound came again.

*It's him. It has to be him.*

*But it can't be.*

Sam jammed her feet into slippers. She'd need them in the freezing January night.

Never had the Phantom come to this side of the river. Was he looking for the pinto mare?

*Please don't let Dad hear me*, she thought, sidestepping the creaky board in the hall. *Or Gram*, she thought, skipping every other step. *Or Brynna.*

*No fair*, she thought, tiptoeing down the last three stairs, *another pair of ears to listen for every move I make.*

When she reached the kitchen, Sam realized the clopping sound wasn't that of advancing hooves. The Phantom—if it was him, and how could it not be?—was pawing at the bridge. Was he anxious? Impatient?

Sam held her breath and turned the doorknob to the right, millimeter by millimeter. It opened onto the porch.

The porch boards wore a thin frosting of snow. No way could she have gone out barefoot. Just the thought made her toes curl. She was so glad she'd put on slippers.

Exhaling slowly, she crept out the door and onto the porch.

An owl hooted in the frosty night. The sound was so near, she expected to see a plume of breath.

If it wasn't for Cougar, she'd leave the door open. It was a windless night. The door wouldn't blow closed and alert the household to her absence.

If she closed it, they might hear.

If she didn't, her tiny kitten could be lost or eaten by a coyote. Or an owl.

Sam pulled it closed. She didn't hear a sound, but the silken rustling of wings told her the owl had heard.

The pawing had stopped. She had to hurry if she was going to see him.

She counted off ten more seconds. If Dad had heard her, he'd be down the stairs by now. She took two steps. Blaze didn't bark from the bunkhouse, and that was good enough for her.

Only a few snowflakes were falling as Sam started down the driveway. Cold clamped on her neck and stabbed through her nightgown, but she kept moving. If the Phantom was on this side of the river, he was here for her.

Animals *did* ask for human help. Even Jake had admitted it on the night the Phantom had allowed her to poultice his injured leg. Why should there be any—

A splash stopped her thoughts. There he was!

A ghost in the night, tail streaming pale against the darkness, he headed for the river.

*Don't go!* She could only shout the words inside her mind. *Zanzibar, I'm here!*

He'd reached the wild side of the river by the time she got to the near shore. La Charla rushed full and steady while the Phantom sped up and down the far bank.

*What is it?* she wanted to ask. The stallion's frenzied gallop threw fresh snow into the air. He wheeled in a haze of icy crystals, then stopped. A cloud of hot breath swirled as he tossed his head in her direction.

What was he doing here alone? Had he left his herd, or had they gone ahead and he'd stayed behind with the dying mare?

*I want to help you.* The ache behind her breastbone turned into a sharp stab.

He was soundless, beautiful. He needed her.

When she did nothing, he turned—not toward the Calico Mountains, but south. He ran toward War Drum Flats.

Like a white feather blowing through snowflakes, he grew smaller and then he was gone.

Sam wrapped her arms around her ribs. He'd given up on her and vanished. Why did it feel like *she* was leaving *him* behind?

Taking careful steps, wishing for the rubber soled boots she kept for winter barn work, Sam recrossed the bridge.

Although she was sad, the white two-story house looked welcoming. With cold winding around her arms and legs, she longed to get back inside. And then she noticed a light upstairs. It hadn't been on before. She was sure of it.

Unless she wanted to freeze, she had no choice. She climbed the porch steps, opened the kitchen door silently, and slid inside.

She stood inside the silent kitchen. There was no movement, no coffee on the stove. Dad hadn't come down yet.

Without him to face, only one thing mattered.

She had to go to the Phantom. But how?

The Calico Mountains were covered with snow. They had been for weeks. But that wouldn't matter if she took the tunnel that cut through the cliffs to the Phantom's secret valley. Just the same, it was unlikely she could get permission to ride up there.

Brynna already had her doing algebra and cleaning her room. What would she do if Sam disobeyed?

It wouldn't be disobeying if she didn't ask, but she hated the guilty feeling of sneaking.

She had to work out a plan. For that, she needed more information.

She could ask Dad, but he had little patience when she talked about mustangs. At best, he'd tell her they'd take care of themselves.

She could ask Jake, but he felt a lot like Dad. Besides, Jake didn't trust her not to get hurt. He panicked each time she hinted she might do something risky. With Jake, it was better to tell him afterward.

So she had to ask Brynna.

Sam nodded. She'd get downstairs and talk with Brynna before she left for Willow Springs. Though Brynna was overdoing her new role as stepmother, she was a wild horse expert. She'd listen to Sam's concerns about the horses and wouldn't dismiss them as childish. After all, Brynna got paid to be paranoid about the mustangs' safety.

Sam stared at the kitchen clock without seeing it. Overhead, she heard a tiny plop, then pinprick patters on the stairs. In the living room, she heard Cougar squeak.

She felt a kind of relief as she lifted him into her arms, then covered him with the knitted blanket Gram kept folded along the back of the couch.

"Stay where it's cozy," Sam told him, though he'd turned into just a bulge moving under the blanket. "I'll be in the kitchen doing algebra forever, so you're not going to miss anything."

Cougar disentangled himself from the blanket. He stretched, arched his back, then opened his mouth in a pink, complaining yawn.

"You don't know how easy you have it," Sam said as she scooped the kitten up and held him under her chin. "You could be living out in the cold, dodging coyotes."

Cougar's purr rumbled in denial, as if no one would make such a cute creature fend for itself.

It was just too cold to sit in the kitchen in her

nightgown. Sam ran upstairs, slipped out of her chilled slippers, and dressed in boots, jeans, and a soft red flannel shirt.

As she came back downstairs, Sam could smell the coffee Dad had made before going outside. How had he slipped down the stairs without her hearing?

Wow. Maybe she'd inherited her stealth from him, because it was a sure thing if Dad had heard her, he wouldn't be quiet about it.

Sam made herself a cup of real cocoa, following the directions on the can. She heated just enough milk for one, in a small saucepan, then measured out the dark brown cocoa powder and sugar. It always seemed weird that you put in a pinch of salt, but Gram said it was a step you shouldn't skip.

When she poured in a bit of hot milk, the mixture looked like fudge. Oh, yum. Sam was more than ready by the time her drink was finished.

Carrying her cup, she settled at the kitchen table, surrounded by lined paper and her algebra textbook. She took up a freshly sharpened pencil and began her work. From outside there came the tinkle and crunch of Dad breaking the ice on Blaze's water bowl and the horses' troughs. It had been a cold night.

She had puzzled through six problems and finished her cocoa when Gram came downstairs.

"Already hard at it, I see," Gram said, kissing Sam's disheveled auburn hair. "Good for you."

"Thanks," Sam said. Even though it seemed like

she'd been up forever, she was pleased at Gram's approval and her twinge of guilt was soothed by the fact that she really was working. "I've got to go meet Jen and work on our project."

Gram placed a black iron skillet on the stove to preheat. She ran water into a kettle and took down a cork-stoppered jar full of oatmeal. Then she turned to Sam.

"Are you going back up to Nugget?" Gram asked.

"We've got that project for Mrs. Ely's class," Sam said absently. This math problem was trickier than the others. She wrote down the page and problem numbers, then glanced up when she noticed there was no sound but the sizzle of melting shortening Gram had scooped into the black skillet. Sam considered Gram's frowning expression. "What?"

"It's all nonsense, of course, based on people who are too careless to watch what they're doing, but you know that old town's supposed to be haunted."

*Well, they do call it a ghost town,* Sam thought. But Gram would take that as sarcasm, so Sam didn't blurt the first thing that came into her mind. Instead, she asked Gram the question she'd been thinking about yesterday.

"Is that why I've never been there? Mrs. Ely says it's a historically significant settlement."

Gram turned off the water she'd been running over some potatoes and dried them before she answered.

"I suppose she's right. It's been there since the Civil War," Gram said. Her chopping knife flew through the potatoes, and she began layering them into the black skillet. "And most of the 'otherworldly' stories could be explained away."

"Like what?" Sam shivered, but she wanted to know.

Gram spent a long time mincing onions and flinging them in with the potatoes before she answered.

"Like ghosts of people who lived there long ago, and spirits of those that went back in our time, looking for wealth someone had left behind."

It had never occurred to Sam that there might still be gold up there. That would be incredible. She could be rich. She and Jen could both be rich. That'd put an end to talk about Jen moving. She could simply buy the ranch back from Slocum.

Sam thought of drilling a second well so Dad would quit worrying about water. Instead, if he wanted to contemplate water at all, he could climb into the hot tub in his bedroom suite, or swim in the pool Sam would build.

But wait. Had Gram just said people had *died* while looking for that left-behind gold? And their spirits . . .

"People haven't really seen ghosts, though, right?" she asked.

"They claim to," Gram said, shrugging. "But what they saw could've been vapor over the hot springs or gas from the mines. You want to be careful of that, in fact," Gram warned. "Poisonous gas is real. When Wyatt was a child, five little boys — his classmates — were playing hide-and-seek there, and died from mine gas poisoning."

Sam thought a minute. She and Jen had been so interested in the lost palomino, they hadn't investigated the gold mines that had given birth to Nugget. She guessed it was a good thing.

"Probably that's as much to blame for why folks around here don't poke around Nugget as often as outsiders do. Vacationers and such seem fascinated by it. But you're a sensible Nevada girl, Samantha. So keep your wits about you while you're exploring."

Sam went back to her work. It wasn't so bad when she could look forward to oatmeal and fried potatoes for breakfast and a ride with Jen. Every school day should be like this.

"Since you're working so hard, I'll bring in the eggs this morning," Gram said. She let the curtain drop from looking out the window.

Sam liked that idea a lot. She didn't want to leave the warm kitchen, but fair was fair. "Wait, Gram. Dad said I still had to do my usual chores."

"I know that," she said. "But from the looks of it, he's already fed the stock. That's one of your chores. Besides, he means for you to clean Ace and Sweetheart's stalls and throw in some fresh straw. And do the same for the run-in shed down at the other end of the ten-acre pasture. With this cold weather, they're spending more time under cover."

"Okay," Sam said. It wasn't the most fun part of being a horse owner, but it wasn't very hard.

"He wants you to scrub a couple of buckets, too, but that's work that would be better done once it warms up a little," Gram said, grabbing the egg basket from its place on top of the refrigerator. "No sense washing them to have them ice up on you."

Gram closed the door behind her and Sam had just turned back to her work when Brynna came into the kitchen.

It was going to take a while to get used to seeing Brynna, BLM executive, wearing a black-and-green plaid bathrobe with her hair streaming loose down her back.

But she wasn't Brynna *Olson* anymore. She was Brynna Forster now, and she had every right to be in the kitchen of River Bend Ranch.

"Coffee," Brynna muttered. She took a blue pottery mug down from the cupboard. She poured, sipped, and sighed, then her eyes popped open. "How are you?" she asked Sam.

"As good as anyone doing algebra can be," Sam replied.

"I know it was my—I mean our—idea, but isn't it a little early for homework?"

"I woke up when it was still dark," Sam said. She considered telling Brynna about her disturbing dreams, but she didn't want to go off on a tangent. "And I decided to get this out of the way so I can go meet Jen at Nugget."

"Okay," Brynna said, but clearly she wasn't paying attention. She lifted the lid on the oatmeal, gave it a stir, then grabbed a carton from the refrigerator and added a stream of milk.

Sam's lips opened to tell her to stop, but she closed them. Gram was awfully fussy about cooking, but maybe Brynna knew what she was doing.

"I wanted to ask you about the horsemeat dealers," Sam said, and Brynna turned so quickly, a lock of red hair spun out and over her shoulder.

"What about them?"

"Are there any?"

Brynna put the lid back on the oatmeal and lifted the one on the frying potatoes before she answered. "We keep getting reports there are, that they're stalking mustangs. I know that with mad cow disease in Europe, consumption of beef is down, but if they're coming here to buy, they're not getting wild horses. The brand inspector keeps close watch for mustangs at the auctions."

Sam realized she'd been chewing the eraser on her pencil while Brynna talked. She put it down on the table, still not satisfied the Phantom was safe.

"If you need something to worry about, make it that mare," Brynna said, and then gasped at her own insensitivity. "That was the wrong thing to say."

Brynna put down her coffee cup and covered one of Sam's hands with one of her own. "I didn't mean you should be worrying. I'm sorry. I know you're concerned for the Phantom and his band."

"I know that for a few days, she ran with his band," Sam said.

Brynna recoiled a little. "For *how* long?"

"Just a few days, that I saw."

"She may have come from another herd," Brynna mused.

"From a band that was sick and, like, maybe she brought the disease with her?"

Brynna was shaking her head. "You never know. She could have been feral."

Brynna's eyes took on a faraway look and her fingers began braiding her hair, almost as if they had minds of their own. She rocked a little in her chair and Sam could tell she was thinking.

Sam's heart didn't want to know what Brynna was mulling over. Her head did. Brynna was a biologist. She'd studied all kinds of things that could go wrong with wildlife.

Sam leaned forward with her arms folded across her book and papers. Algebra forgotten, she watched her stepmother. At last, Brynna's eyes refocused. Head tilted to one side, she said, "There is something I'd forgotten all about. I'd have to do more, study . . ."

Sam swallowed hard, then asked, "What is it?"

"The fatal white factor," Brynna said. "It's a

genetic condition. I'm sure you've heard of it."

Sam's chest tightened. She pictured the Phantom as a long-legged black foal learning to stand in River Bend's warm barn. Her imagination showed him turning into a young gray. Now, he was silver and soon, very soon, he'd be completely white.

## Chapter Eight

"I've heard of the fatal white factor," Sam said. She tried to push back a wave of dizziness. "But what is it, exactly?"

"Nothing for you to worry about," Brynna said. She took a deep breath. "I just keep saying the wrong thing, don't I?"

"But I want to know," Sam insisted.

Brynna nodded as if she understood.

"As I remember, it only occurs in all-white foals of pinto parents."

The Phantom's father was a gray and his mother was sorrel, but Sam kept listening.

"*Foals,*" Brynna said with emphasis, "with this condition, are born with an intestinal problem. I am sorry, Sam. It just popped into my mind when I was thinking about that pinto mare. I didn't mean to give you something else to worry about."

For a minute it was quiet. There was one last,

ugly thing Sam had to ask about the dead mare. When she finally did, Sam found she couldn't ask it above a whisper.

"Did they just leave her out there?"

Right away, Brynna knew what Sam meant.

"Jake's dad and brothers picked her up. She's being examined by state vets to see what happened."

"Okay," Sam said. She didn't want to know any more, and felt a moment of worry when Brynna tossed her loosely braided hair back over her shoulder and went on.

"Look, if there were any defects in the Phantom's herd, they would have shown up long before now. As far as I can see, the only things your horse is transmitting to his herd are speed, beauty, and—since they've managed to outwit mustangers for so long—intelligence."

Sam couldn't help smiling. It felt like Brynna had given her a personal compliment. How weird, Sam thought, that Brynna was giving her more support than her best friend.

Brynna pushed away from the table just as Gram came back into the kitchen carrying a big box.

"I got a present for Sweetheart in New Mexico," Gram said. "It was too big to carry home on the plane, so I mailed it home." Gram gestured toward the sound of a retreating vehicle. "They just dropped it off."

Gram used a paring knife to slit open the box. She

folded back the flaps and lifted out a purple and turquoise horse blanket decorated with angular white hearts.

"Handwoven," Gram said. "I am such a fool over that old horse, but I figured if I liked to keep my old bones cozy in the wintertime, so would she."

Both Sam and Brynna admired the blanket, until Gram folded it back into its box, set it aside, and turned to the stove.

"I'd better get dressed for work," Brynna said, but she turned back.

"It's Saturday," Sam said. "Do you have to go in?"

"I have some catching up to do," Brynna said. "Besides, they might have some results on that mare. They were supposed to fax them over immediately. You know Sam, we could have missed something very simple."

While Brynna was upstairs, Sam worked to finish her math. She was almost done when Gram clanged a pot lid back on.

"Samantha, what have I told you about patience?" Gram demanded. "A good cook doesn't rush food."

Sam had no idea why Gram was yelling at her. Her bewilderment must have shown on her face.

"These potatoes," Gram said, pointing, "are pale as fish bellies. They needed to fry another five minutes, at least, before you turned them. Now they're crunchy on one side and limp on the other."

Sam felt a surge of anger at Gram's injustice, but she took the blame. Brynna was having a tough enough time fitting in without Sam tattling that she'd been the one who'd meddled with breakfast.

Boots stamped on the porch, then Dad came in. By the alert way he surveyed the two of them, Sam could tell he'd heard Gram's voice. He didn't say anything, though, just brushed some straw from his shirtsleeve.

The movement startled Sam and she wondered if it was Brynna's influence. Dad rarely thought about looking tidy.

Gram picked up another pot lid, then slammed it back down.

"And heavens, girl, it's not that I don't appreciate the help, but what did you do to this oatmeal?"

Gram scooped up a wooden spoonful of the cereal. A gluey glop dripped off the spoon and back into the saucepan. "It's not fit to eat."

"It was me, Grace," Brynna confessed, as she strode back into the kitchen.

She looked efficient and professional in her khaki uniform, but each word in the sentence dwindled.

As if she felt her confidence fading, Brynna took one long step to the sink and rinsed her coffee cup. Without putting it down, she dried it and returned it to the cupboard.

"I have to go in early," Brynna said. "I'll call if I learn anything about that mare. Sam, some of those old mining areas are really dangerous. Mine shafts, contaminated groundwater . . ." Brynna made a wide gesture. "Nugget's been the scene of some nasty accidents."

"I'm always careful," Sam promised.

One corner of Brynna's mouth rose in a skeptical smile and Sam wished Dad or Gram would rush in and convince Brynna everything was fine. Instead, Gram made herself super busy at the stove and Dad just let Brynna keep going.

"I've read real documentation—not gossip—on a man who broke both legs when the ground beneath him gave way, up there."

"I wouldn't walk anyplace that looked unsafe," Sam began.

"On the surface," Brynna warned as she smoothed one hand through the air, "it looks completely normal. Underneath, it's honeycombed with tunnels."

Brynna watched Dad as she added, "And if Ace hesitates to drink, trust his instincts."

Dad nodded in agreement, but apparently that wasn't enough for Brynna. She strode across the kitchen and had her hand on the doorknob, ready to leave, when she turned back. "I don't think it's a safe place for you to be."

Sam took a deep breath. Everyone knew she was going up there for school, not for fun, so what was the problem?

"Are you saying I can't go?" Sam asked.

Brynna's eyes flew to Dad's.

"You'd know if we were saying that," Dad told her. "Just stay sensible."

"I will," Sam said. "And Gram told me the chores you want me to do. I'll get started as soon as I change."

Then, before Dad added more chores to the list or launched into another lecture, she hurried upstairs.

Sam rushed through her chores and called Jen to ask her to ride out as far as the bus stop to meet her. They agreed to bring their lunches, so they could spend plenty of time in Nugget without getting hungry.

But Sam had one more detail to take care of before she left the house. She called Jake.

Sam didn't really expect Jake to answer. It was ten-thirty, and by this time, she was pretty sure he'd be out working on the irrigation system. But there were seven Ely brothers and two parents, so Sam figured someone should be around to answer the phone. She just hoped it wouldn't be Jake's mom. Although she was really nice, and had known her since she was born, their conversations often felt a little awkward, because Jake's mom was also Mrs. Ely, Sam's history teacher.

"Hi Samantha," Mrs. Ely greeted her. "Jake tells me you're working on your history project."

"Yes, ma'am, we are," Sam said. "I'm just about to

go meet Jennifer Kenworthy. She's my partner."

"I remember," Mrs. Ely said. "Are things going all right?"

"Well . . ."

"Your Dad's not giving you a hard time about going up there, is he? I went myself just a few weeks ago to check it out. There's no way I'd send any of my students somewhere dangerous."

"I think Brynna's more worried than Dad," Sam said. She felt a little disloyal, but it wouldn't hurt to let Mrs. Ely know she was determined to get the project finished with or without parental support. Maybe she'd think Sam deserved extra high marks for extra hard effort.

"I'll have a talk with her," Mrs. Ely suggested.

For a minute, Sam thought that might work. Then she reconsidered. Dad liked Mrs. Ely a lot, but he thought she was a little bossy.

"You know, I think we're working it out," Sam said.

"That's probably for the best," Mrs. Ely said simply. "So, I bet you didn't call about the project. Although I can't help but remind you the artifact and accompanying notes are due Monday. And when you do that map, make sure you mark the spot where the artifact was gathered. I want it returned. Nugget isn't recognized by the state as an historic site yet, but when it is, I don't want my students to be responsible for removing significant relics. Then the mapping and field notes are turned in on Friday."

Sam's head was spinning. Even though she knew all of this, it was different hearing it directly from the teacher. She took a deep breath to respond. Before she could, Mrs. Ely's voice turned unteacherly.

"But I bet you called to talk with Jake."

"I did, actually," Sam said. "Could you have him call me later?"

"Sure," Mrs. Ely said. "But he already said he wanted to borrow his dad's truck and drive over to River Bend tonight. Something about math homework? Hard to believe on a Saturday night, and you can imagine how his brothers were harassing him about it."

She could imagine it, and she was surprised Jake had already planned this. He couldn't possibly know what she wanted to talk about.

After Sam had said good-bye and hung up the phone, she wondered, not for the first time, whether Jake Ely was psychic, or just knew her way too well.

Every minute of the ride toward Nugget, Sam breathed in the cold winter air and watched for the Phantom. The thin layer of snow had vanished from the flats, but it still clung to the shady side of the foothills and she was glad she'd worn thermal underwear beneath her shirt and jeans.

Sam's eyes skimmed the pine-studded ridge tops, the deer paths, and wind-scrubbed sky. As she searched for the wild mustang, she tried to absorb the sights and store them up. In a few days, she'd ache to be back out here instead of back at school, confined by classroom walls.

As she and Jen rode past the trail to Lost Canyon, she looked carefully. Arroyo Azul lay in the bottom of the canyon, and several times she'd seen the Phantom headed that way. But not today.

Jen, wearing a bulky pink ski jacket decorated with snowflakes, didn't seem to mind Sam's preoccupation. In fact, they were nearly to Nugget by the time Jen blurted a question she'd probably been mulling over all day.

"Why is she there?"

Sam knew Jen had to mean Golden Rose, but she didn't get a chance to answer.

"I mean, I'm glad she's in Nugget, because she might be there again today, but horses are social animals. Why wouldn't she be with a herd?"

Jen's head was tilted to one side as she waited for Sam to answer.

"I've sort of been wondering, too. And she looked clean. You said she's been missing for more than two years, right?" Sam paused as Jen nodded. "But Jen, her mane wasn't even tangled."

"It doesn't make sense. I didn't notice her feet, did you?" Jen asked, clearly thinking that if the mare's hooves had been trimmed, she hadn't been running wild all this time. "She was prancing, but I think that's her natural gait."

All at once, Sam slowed Ace to a gentle jog. "Here's where we saw the mirage yesterday. I wonder if we'll see it again."

As Jen looked skyward, the lenses of her glasses reflected the gray bellies of the clouds. "The weather's not nearly so bright."

"You did see the horse in the mirage, didn't you?" Sam asked.

"What?" Jen's mouth quirked up at one corner. "This is why you're good at creative stuff at school. I only saw upside-down buildings. Weren't they enough for you?"

"Well, I thought I saw a horse." Sam said it hesitantly, though she was positive of what she'd seen.

"You just wanted to see a horse," Jen assured her. "You're always looking for the Phantom. Come on, let's gallop a little. I want to have plenty of time to find Rose and do our project." Jen caught Sam's concerned touch on Ace's neck. "They'll have time to cool out once we start up the grade into Nugget."

"I know I was just going off about your imagination," Jen said as they reached the main street of Nugget. "But doesn't it feel different than before? Like someone's here?"

It did. Sam felt Ace quiver beneath her, and then he neighed.

"Another horse," Sam said as she recognized Ace's greeting. "Gotta be."

"Let's try that garden," Jen whispered.

A feeling like electricity, almost of being watched, streaked down the nape of Sam's neck and she nodded at Jen.

As if they understood, Ace and Silly took quiet steps to the right side of the street, passed the abandoned schoolhouse with its silent bell, then stopped as they reached the stark garden.

It was empty, but both horses' heads lifted. Their ears pricked and their nostrils worked. Sam glanced toward the ravine. Nothing, but—

"Listen," Jen mouthed the word and held a mittened hand beside her ear.

Creaking. The sound of unoiled hinges came faintly to them. They wouldn't have heard a thing if the horses had been moving. And it could just be the wind, but then, suddenly, there was the tick of something hard hitting wood and then muffled thuds.

The image took only seconds to fill Sam's mind. It sounded like a horse going over a jump.

"Go!" she hissed at Jen, but she'd already sent Silly after the sound.

They swung the horses around the edge of the schoolhouse, back onto the main street.

"This is ridiculous!" Sam snapped when there was no horse on the street, no horse lunging up any of the hillsides. In fact, she saw no movement at all until she looked toward the cemetery. There, a black raven, big as a beagle, stood cawing next to a sagging wooden headstone.

Reacting to their riders' indecision, both horses kept their front hooves propped while their back legs danced, shifting from side to side.

"Go on, girl," Jen urged Silly. "Find her."

"If they'd even caught a glimpse of her," Sam complained, "that whole herd instinct would have kicked in, but I don't think they know where she's gone."

Jen made a sound a lot like a growl. "And anything in town could have made that creaking sound."

It was true. Ahead, one bare cottonwood branch rubbed against another. Behind them, a shutter on the schoolhouse moved, and over to the left, a rusty chain had broken, but still suspended a wooden sign.

"We'd better get to work," Sam said, but Jen was still surveying the town, shaking her head.

"I have to find her," Jen insisted.

"What we have to find is artifacts. This assignment—"

"You look," Jen said, whirling Silly away from Ace. "I'm going to check out that ravine. That's where she went before."

"Je-en," Sam heard her voice pull her friend's name out in a beseeching way. She didn't want to be left alone here.

Jen sighed, as if she at least understood. Then, she pushed her glasses up on her nose with an impatient index finger. Then she glanced at her watch.

"Give me thirty minutes."

Sam could tell it wouldn't be worth her breath to argue, so she stayed quiet.

Just then the raven croaked three times and Sam gave a nervous laugh.

"Good thing I don't believe in omens," she said.

"Oh, don't be such a baby," Jen scolded her. "You'll be fine."

"That's what they all say," Sam shouted as Jen rode away. "In horror movies," she added, as Silly's white tail vanished around the corner of the schoolhouse. "And then . . ." Sam yelled louder, but she heard only her echo and Silly's hooves clattering on the rock-strewn path into the ravine.

Besides, what happened in horror movies when someone was left all alone didn't bear thinking about.

## Chapter Nine

"Okay," Sam told Ace as she dismounted and ground-tied him. "I'm not going to do all the work for both of us."

Ace swung his head around to watch her loosen his cinch. His head bobbed.

"Yeah, see," Sam said. "You wouldn't do it all either, would you?"

Ace blew through his lips, losing interest. He stamped a front hoof, then turned back and loudly worked his tongue against his bit.

"I get the hint," Sam said and eased the gentle curb bit from his mouth.

What she would do, Sam decided, was scope out the places she deemed most likely to have interesting and portable artifacts.

She scanned this side of the street. General store. Assay office. Sheriff's office. Icehouse. Battle-Born Saloon.

She didn't want to go inside any of them alone, but she had nothing to fear, not really.

"General store," she pronounced loudly. Mrs. Ely wanted them to compare and contrast what they found with modern life. She was certainly familiar with a modern grocery store, so this would be the easiest place to start.

The store lacked a door. As she stood in the place one might have hung, she wished she'd brought Blaze along. But Jen calling her a baby still stung, so she drew a deep breath and stepped inside.

The store didn't have a single window, so it was dark as night. Sam's hand moved instinctively for a light switch, but she caught herself before she touched anything. Instead, she stood with both arms crossed over her notebook, waiting for her eyes to adjust to the shadows.

She let her other senses take over. It was colder in here than it was outside. That would make it fine in the summer, but in the winter, there'd better be a stove to keep people warm. She took a careful sniff of the air. At first she smelled only dust, but then caught the scent of some herb that smelled like a combination of black pepper and oregano.

She took one careful step and felt the boards beneath her boots bend. Someone had cared enough to put in a wooden floor, but it hadn't stayed flat.

A big solid table sat in the middle of the store. She could imagine someone rolling out cloth to be measured there. Or maybe stacking provisions, counting them up and tallying their cost for a miner moving on to California.

She blinked and noticed broken shelves slanting across one wall. One end was still attached, but the other ended in an avalanche of cans and broken bottles on the floor. She didn't see any whole bottles. Maybe, before Nugget's gate was in place, bottle collectors had come in and taken the relics.

Using her toe, Sam nudged a couple of cans. Next time she'd bring the flashlight in with her. She didn't really want to touch one of the cans if they weren't bringing them in for class.

"Okay," she said. And though her voice was quiet, it might as well have boomed.

She turned back toward the door and gasped as spiderwebs floated before her eyes. No. She took a step back and looked upward. Here near the door she could see that the rafters were festooned with cobwebs, as if decorated for a Halloween party. She just knew they'd be sticky, and the idea of getting them in her hair was creepy.

Sam sidled out the door. When she exhaled so loudly that Ace looked up with an answering snort, Sam wondered if she'd been holding her breath.

She walked over, lifted Ace's head, and kissed him on the nose.

"Good boy," she said, but when the gelding pulled away she realized she wasn't comforting him at all.

She was comforting herself.

Proving to herself she wasn't scared, she bypassed everything until she reached the Battle-Born Saloon. From the street yesterday, she hadn't noticed that slats of absolutely modern plywood had been hammered to form a sort of lattice over the window.

"Shoot, and Mrs. Ely is worried about *us* moving pieces of glass and stuff," she muttered.

All the same, Sam managed to see inside, because the window let some light into the cavernous room and way in the back, the glow of more light wavered in bars. Squinting, she didn't see the long mahogany bar or crystal chandeliers she was expecting. Over in the corner, though—Sam moved a little closer—that might be the remains of a player piano.

Oh, wow! What a great artifact that would make!

She could almost imagine tinkly Western music.

"Buffalo gals won't you come out tonight, come out tonight, come out tonight." She murmured the only saloon song she knew and tried not to imagine ghoulish gamblers and the spirits of dancing girls frolicking to her tune.

Ghosts or not, she was going in.

Sam moved to the saloon's swinging doors and gingerly shoved them with her shoulder.

Sam stepped back and looked at them. They sure didn't swing anymore. In fact, they felt so solid, she wondered if they were bolted or nailed closed from inside. And something in there smelled like hay.

Hay? That couldn't be right, but she was determined to find something interesting to brag about when Jen returned. That meant she had to go in there.

Actually, the familiar scent of hay convinced her it wouldn't be so creepy inside.

Sam squatted and peered under the doors. Hay was strewn over the wooden floor, which was probably like the one in the general store underneath.

It didn't smell as dusty and neglected as the store, but maybe there was just less stuff in there. Sam sawed her lip against her teeth.

"Do it," Sam ordered herself, then held her breath as she lowered her head and duck-walked under the doors.

She was inside. Sam stood slowly. "Okay, I did it."

As she had before, Sam let her eyes grow accustomed to the darkness. This place was brighter. With her gaze fixed on the bulky dark object that really did look like a player piano, she took a step.

Suddenly, the floor caved in with a splintering crash. Boards grabbed at her boots, clawed at her calves, then suddenly she was up to her knees in the saloon floor.

She didn't scream, exactly, but Sam heard the echo of her own squawk.

She wasn't the only one, either. Tiny toe-nailed feet scurried nearby and overhead dark wings fluttered.

Bats. Sam closed her eyes and fisted her hands. She would not cover her head. Bats didn't fly into your hair. They had radar, right?

But what lay under this saloon? She was knee-deep in whatever it was, and though the rats didn't scare her much, she didn't want terrified rodents darting up her pant leg. Or snakes.

Rattlesnakes hibernated in the winter in a big, cozy, poisonous ball.

Sam lunged upward, aware that she was swinging her arms in a way that was just as useless as the weird keening sound forcing through her lips.

Only when she'd jerked loose of the boards and raced back toward the light did she see what had happened. She studied the strewn straw and splintered boards. More plywood, modern wood, right in that spot, not like the rest of the floor at all.

Someone had purposely replaced a section of floor with plywood that would collapse under a weight as light as hers.

No, wait—maybe the plywood covered treasure. Sam stood on tiptoe and peered in. It looked as if the dirt beneath the floor had been dug out a little, but there were no old canvas moneybags spilling gold coins. In fact, there was nothing but dirt.

The floor had been booby-trapped.

And now Sam knew why. She smelled horses.

Stepping carefully, testing each inch of floor before she let her weight down, Sam made her way toward the light in the rear of the saloon. A glow from outside surrounded the player piano and fresh wood showed where the old finish and years of grime had been cut away. Rats didn't inflict damage like that, but a cribbing horse did.

Behind the piano lay fresh straw and a bucket. Rails that had blocked the open wall were scattered on the floor.

Sam knew she was looking at a makeshift stall. She knew why Golden Rose hadn't looked wild and tangled. But Sam's discovery had solved one mystery and created another.

If the last of the Kenworthy palominos had been a captive for two years, who had been her jailer?

## Chapter Ten

Sam spent about ten minutes searching the makeshift stall for clues. If there were any, she decided, it would take a professional to find them. She'd hoped for a rope or halter, even a feed sack, but she found nothing. Whoever came to tend Golden Rose was careful not to leave hints to his identity.

Except for tracks.

Jake had given her a few tips on reading tracks, but the skill remained as much a challenge to her as did algebra. Still, as Sam stood in the straw and peered out through the open back of the saloon, she saw two sets of hoofprints. Only one set was shod.

Jake could have read the tracks like a road sign. After a minute or two of study, he would have known when the tracks were made, the weight of the rider, and how fast the horse was traveling.

Sam could only pick her way around the tracks to keep from obliterating them.

When she returned to Ace, she found him a few feet from where she'd left him, half asleep. The little bay mustang stood with one rear hoof cocked and eyelids drooping. "Getting bored?" she asked, but Ace ignored her.

Because her horse was so sleepy, she probably shouldn't worry that he'd wander off. But she had visions of Jen herding a galloping Golden Rose back into Nugget. Even though Ace had learned to live with humans, he was a mustang. His urge to run was strong. She didn't want to test it against his training.

She could tie him, but the only hitching rail was near a watering trough. The water inside almost had to be rainwater, and certainly pure, but Sam refused to take a chance. Brynna had warned her not to water horses here. If she did anything to harm Ace, she'd never forgive herself.

While Ace dozed, Sam listened. It had been nearly an hour since Jen left. She'd promised to be back by now, but Sam was pretty sure Jen hadn't been hurt. She was just carried away by the chase. Sam wasn't worried, but she was eager to show Jen the stall and get her best guess on who'd kept Golden Rose confined here.

Could it be a clue that yesterday, she and Jen had met up with Jake and Ryan, both riding shod horses near Nugget?

As soon as Jake popped into her mind, Sam thought of his mother, Mrs. Ely.

She swallowed a moan. She and Jen still didn't have an artifact, let alone a map of where they'd found it.

Since she was standing right in front of the store labeled *Ice*, she decided to go inside. She wondered where the ice had come from. Maybe during the little town's glory days, blocks of ice had been cut from the La Charla River and carried this far by horse-drawn wagon.

She fidgeted a minute as she looked at the tilted gray doorway. There was nothing to fear in there, she was sure. There shouldn't be much inside to attract mice. Or snakes, or any other kind of animal she'd be afraid to face.

She felt confident she'd be alone in the ice shop, but she wondered about traps. Surely the one in the saloon had only been dug to keep out people who might find Golden Rose.

If the keeper of Golden Rose had sabotaged this place, too, he'd be sorry. Sam considered herself a nice person, but those moments in the saloon, when she'd imagined snakes coiling around her ankles, had been terrifying. If she felt that way again, she'd hunt down whoever was doing this and show him how it felt to be scared.

Standing in the doorway to the icehouse, Sam was really glad she'd been feeling paranoid. Although it looked like every other structure from outside, inside it was completely different.

The icehouse floor was about five feet lower than the doorway. If she'd just sauntered through the door, she would have taken a hard fall. At least she would have landed on sawdust, though.

That's what reminded her of what she already knew. In the old days, they'd piled blocks of ice up to floor level. They'd covered the blocks with sawdust to absorb the water. The back portion of the little building was for doing business, so the floor there was at ground level.

That part of the store was cluttered with some kind of furniture. She couldn't quite tell what, because of the darkness, but it looked like there was a back door, too. Maybe business was done out the back door.

Feeling brave because she hadn't been tricked, Sam jumped down to the floor and started looking around. The remains of a wooden table that had crumbled away from three of its four legs leaned against the right-hand wall. She guessed it had fallen from the upper level.

Trapped between the tilted tabletop and the rock wall was what she'd been looking for all along. She just hadn't known it.

Sam's fear fell away at the sight of an old newspaper. She and Jen would have the coolest artifact of all. Yellowed with age and brittle, the newspaper had already broken into fragments. She couldn't tell if it had been a single sheet of newsprint, or more.

Using her fingers as carefully as if they were tweezers, Sam lifted each delicate piece of paper and slid it into the plastic bag Mrs. Ely had recommended she bring.

Even though the largest pieces were about the size of her palm, Sam couldn't tell if this was a local newspaper, printed and distributed in Nugget, or something left behind by a traveler. Either way, it would be fun to reassemble it like a jigsaw puzzle.

When she'd lifted all the pieces bigger than dust, she sealed the bag.

She was feeling pretty proud of herself when she realized the jump down to the icehouse floor had been easier than the climb up would be.

Sam tilted her head up and surveyed the ground-level floor. She could climb up there and go out the back door more easily than the front door, if she could slip past the jumble of furniture.

Holding the plastic bag in her teeth, Sam used the rocks in the wall as steps and the edge of the floor for handholds. She swung up almost as easily as if she'd been mounting a horse.

"Piece of cake," she said, though she doubted anyone would have recognized the words, which had to work past her teeth and the bag.

Blinking into the darkness, she could see that the furniture was piled like a barricade in front of the door.

Except it wasn't furniture.

Sam's heart beat faster. Chills rushed down her arms as her body recognized the shapes before her mind did.

*They're —*

*No. They're too small.*

Shaking her head, Sam tried to come up with another use for rectangular wooden boxes. She couldn't, because her stomach made a sickening plummet. She knew exactly what they were. Coffins.

The shiver that shook her might have been caused by all the ice piled in here a hundred years ago.

Why were there coffins in the icehouse?

It was bad enough thinking that they were here so that their contents wouldn't decompose in the desert heat. It was worse, far worse, that they were so small.

"They're empty."

Startled by her own voice and the bag falling from her teeth, Sam jumped. She steadied herself against the rock wall so that she wouldn't fall back to the lowered floor.

Of course they were empty. Slowly, she bent and retrieved the plastic bag by touch. All the while, she kept her eyes on the coffins.

*As if they're going to do what?* she mocked herself silently. The wooden lids weren't going to creak open and snap closed on her wrist. No weird supernatural gravity would suck her inside and keep her there.

They were just old wooden boxes.

She could hear the wind outside, the gentle ping of the bell at the abandoned schoolhouse, and the sound of Ace's hooves shifting on the dirt street. This was real life, not the horror movie she'd thought of as Jen rode away.

Sam concentrated on a skinny opening between the two stacks of coffins. Placing her boots heel to toe, she might make it through without knocking them over. Creepy or not, the caskets were valuable. If she knocked them to the sawdust-covered floor below, they'd break apart.

"Take it easy," Sam told herself.

Even as she stepped between the caskets, balancing like she was on a tightrope, she wondered why Ace was so restless, out on the street.

Her boot heel touched her boot toe. Almost out. Another step. Another.

Almost there. Two more steps and she breathed fresh air. All she had to do was duck through the doorway and she'd be safe.

Cobwebs trailed against her cheek as she bolted free of the icehouse.

Outside, Sam stood for a minute with her hands on her hips. Then, ignoring the raucous raven in the graveyard, she returned to Ace. With the greatest care, she slid the plastic bag containing the newspaper fragments into her saddlebags.

She'd just buckled the bag closed when she heard Jen's scream.

"I'm coming!" Sam shouted once, then bolted toward the ravine.

Clumsy in her boots, she ran just the same, over the dusty stone paths through the abandoned garden. Once her boot sole skidded and she almost fell. She slowed just a little. She'd be no good to Jen with a broken ankle.

In the winter light, the ravine glowed rust-purple. For a second, Sam thought she heard a whisper of water among the cascade of rocks, but the sound was quickly covered by a voice.

"I'm okay," Jen shouted.

Sam's eyes hunted and found her friend. She was afoot.

"Now you tell me," Sam gasped.

About halfway up the boulder-littered path, Jen held Silly's reins with the big mare dancing at the end of them. Her ears pointed forward, but she looked to one side, eyes rolled to show the whites. She acted as if there was so much to fear, she couldn't focus on just one thing.

Sam didn't allow herself to relax. She knew Jen hadn't screamed because she'd fallen off her horse.

"What happened?" Sam shouted as she kept walking, arms out, balancing as she picked her way over the big rocks.

"Come look."

Jen's skin was no paler than usual, but she looked sick. When she forced a smile, her lips trembled.

"It's no big deal," Jen managed. "I'm truly embarrassed. You can check with my parents to verify this, but I don't believe that I've ever, in my entire life, screamed." Jen pushed her glasses up on her nose. She threw one white-blond braid over her shoulder, then did the same with the other. "Maybe because it's a ghost town. . . ."

"Jen, it doesn't matter. Something startled you," Sam began making an excuse for her friend. "It happens."

"Oh, no. 'Startled' isn't it," Jen said, still wearing that queasy expression. "Look."

Grabbing a leaf-bare sapling for balance, Sam climbed up a little higher so she could peer in the direction Jen pointed.

The white, blade-shaped object was a bone, but Sam didn't recognize it as a shoulder until she spotted another part of the skeleton nearby. Leaning against an ocher-yellow boulder, with eye sockets dark and staring, was a horse skull.

Sam swallowed hard, then glanced up the ravine, wondering if the horse had fallen. "Maybe it was running from a predator, and with all these rocks—"

"I don't think that's likely. I'm afraid something else is going on," Jen said. She took a deep, shuddering breath. "Take a look at this."

Wrinkling her nose, Jen squatted and moved her index finger in a floating circle above the speckled brown body of a ground squirrel.

As if her mistress had reawakened her early terror, Silly squealed and yanked at the reins, pulling Jen over backward.

Jen rolled on her side and shoved to her feet.

"Just knock it off!" she shouted, giving the reins a sharp tug.

Surprised, Sam started to tell Jen that hurting Silly was no way to make her settle down. But Jen knew that.

"You've already proven you're the dumbest horse around today," Jen said as Silly's hooves scrabbled and her forefeet lifted a few inches off the ground. "Do you know what she did?" Jen said over her shoulder. "We were within *yards* of Rose, and idiot girl here pinned her ears, lashed her tail, and started backing around like she wanted to kick!"

*Maybe Silly was jealous*, Sam thought, but she only said, "And Rose took off?"

"Of course she took off!"

While Jen continued to scold her mare, Sam looked away. Jen would never hurt Silly, but she might take out her embarrassment over her scream on the palomino.

"Do you really think that's helping?" Sam asked. Then, she returned her gaze to the ground squirrel, but she heard Jen's frustrated sigh.

*What could kill both horses and ground squirrels*? Sam wondered.

The skeleton was from a horse long dead, but the

squirrel must have died recently. *Very* recently, she thought, or it would have been eaten by a coyote or other scavenger.

"I'm not bringing you next time. Do you hear?" Jen asked Silly.

Next time, she might know exactly where to find Golden Rose, Sam thought. Next time, the mare might be standing in a stall, just waiting for them to take her home.

"Jen," Sam said, touching her friend's arm. "I know where Golden Rose has been all this time."

"Oh sure, where?" Jen asked skeptically.

"In the Battle-Born Saloon." Sam gestured toward Nugget's main street.

Jen's pale eyebrows rose higher than the top of her glasses frames.

"Really," Sam said. "I know where, and I know how she was kept there," Sam said smugly.

Just then a rock tumbled down from the highest point in the ravine. When Sam looked up, she saw a rider silhouetted on the rim.

"And now," she said on an indrawn breath, "I think I know by *who*."

## Chapter Eleven

Ryan Slocum rode tall in his English saddle. He swayed only slightly as Sky picked his way down through massive boulders that looked like a frozen avalanche.

"Are you all right?" he inquired. "I happened past and thought I heard a cry for help."

Jen groaned with embarrassment, but Sam ignored her.

All of this weird stuff had an explanation. That explanation was Ryan Slocum. When the ghost town's school bell had rung yesterday to distract her and Jen, Ryan had rung it, then taken some back way out. When the beautiful Kenworthy palomino had inexplicably hung around Nugget, she'd been kept captive by Ryan. And the booby traps —

Sam's thoughts were stopped by a red wall of anger.

Although she was on foot and he soared above

her on the dark brown gelding, Sam shook her fist at Ryan Slocum.

"It's you!" Sam shouted. "Admit it!"

"I'm not certain I understand," Ryan's lilting English accent only made his fake puzzlement more irritating.

"Oh yes, you do!" Sam yelled.

Brightness broke through the clouds, and afternoon sun shone directly behind Ryan's head. No matter how much she squinted, Sam couldn't quite focus on his face because of the glare. It made her madder still.

"Sam," Jen's tone cautioned her friend not to go completely nuts.

It didn't help.

"Don't fall for this innocent act, Jen. I can't believe how brazen he's been!" Sam shook her head in amazement. "He's living practically next door to you, right on the very same ranch. The *Kenworthy* ranch, from which the last of the Kenworthy palominos disappeared, and all along, he's had her."

Ryan sat his horse quietly, allowing Sam to hear the flaw in her argument.

"Uh, Sam?" Jen said quietly. "Rose has been missing two years. He's only been here two *months*."

"I don't care," Sam insisted. Thinking of the awful instant when she'd feared she'd fallen into a hundred rattlesnakes' hibernation den, she didn't back down. "You didn't just happen by here yesterday, did you?" Sam demanded. "You're the one who's been keeping

Jen's horse in that makeshift stall."

Ryan sighed. "Actually, I thought that for an improvised pen, it was rather clever."

He'd admitted it.

Sam whirled to look at Jen. Her friend's studious expression was better suited to the mysteries of mathematics than Ryan's revelation. True to his Slocum bloodlines, he was obviously an unscrupulous jerk.

In the silence that followed Ryan's admission, Ace's lonely nicker rang out from down below. With a cautious glance at Jen, Silly answered. Her call echoed from side to side in the ravine.

"In the old days, they used to hang horse thieves," Sam snapped.

Ryan gave her the kind of half smile you'd give an amusing child.

"Shall we continue our discussion down below?" Ryan formed it as a question, but he was already leading the way.

Sam huffed. She would have stomped, too, but she didn't want to fall. She took a last look at the horse skull and ground squirrel corpse and wondered how they fit into all this.

Ace trotted around the corner of the schoolhouse to greet Silly.

*So much for ground-tying*, Sam thought. But she couldn't blame Ace. A lot of strange stuff was going on and when Silly called, he'd acted like the social animal he was.

She didn't scold him; just let him touch noses with

Silly, then snagged his reins and followed the others back to Nugget's main street.

Once they were down, Sam walked right past Ryan. She couldn't help but notice that Jen lagged behind, nearer Ryan than she was to her best friend.

*You'll see*, Sam thought. *Ryan Slocum may be cute, but he's a big fat liar.*

Sam stood beside Ace. She stroked his neck as she watched slimy Ryan Slocum try to wriggle out of a full confession.

"Surely you aren't saying I've *rustled* your horse?" Ryan nodded toward Silly.

"Not that palomino," Sam snapped. "The other one. Golden Rose."

Again, Sam glanced toward Jen and waited for backup.

Jen tidied a few tendrils of her blond hair, tucking them back into her braids. She straightened her pink parka and wet her lips.

"I really have no idea what's come over her," Jen said in a bewildered voice.

Her. Her *who*?

Jen couldn't be apologizing to Ryan for her, but it sounded as if that's exactly what she was doing. So, Sam stood up for herself.

"All that's 'come over' me," Sam said, "is the realization that he's been keeping Golden Rose in a stall in the Battle-Born Saloon, and he booby-trapped the entrance so that I fell."

For the first time, Sam glanced down at the leg that had been quietly aching.

"He made me rip my newest boot-cut jeans, and I could have broken my leg, or my neck or . . ." Sam ran out of breath before she could finish.

Apparently all the facts she'd thrown at him convinced Ryan to surrender.

"The palomino mare is yours? The dark-skinned one that's been hanging about here?"

Jen's mouth was agape.

*Why am I doing all the arguing here?* Sam wondered. *And why is Jen swallowing Ryan Slocum's lies?*

Ace faced Sam, sending her equine ESP with his intelligent, wide-set eyes. If she hadn't been so angry, Sam would have laughed. Ace's expression urged Sam to keep after the unashamed horse thief.

"Don't give me that, Ryan Slocum," Sam reprimanded him. "Rose wasn't 'hanging about.' You kept her in that stall."

"I thought she was a mustang," he said, but Sam noticed he studied his rein hand as he said it. "I admit she seemed an awfully tractable wild horse."

"And you dug that pit and—"

"I wasn't trying to steal her." Ryan lifted his chin, then flushed to the roots of his shining coffee-brown hair. "Honestly."

"Maybe you weren't certain she belonged to someone," Sam said. "But I bet you suspected."

"It doesn't matter," Jen rushed in.

"Doesn't matter?" Sam yelped.

"I just want her back, so I can give her to my dad." Jen sounded as if she might cry. Sam looked away.

The winter sun that had shone so brightly above the rim of the ravine looked cold and flat as an old dime. It was slipping down toward the horizon. As it did, Nugget fell into shadows and Sam could have sworn the temperature dropped ten degrees.

"Jen, we'd better get going," Sam told her.

"Yeah," Jen said, but she didn't mount up.

"Briefly, I'll tell you how it came about," Ryan said. "Just after I arrived, I rode up here, exploring, and glimpsed the most exquisite palomino. She was almost Arabic in her lines." Ryan paused when Jen nodded in recognition. "At first, it was difficult to get near her. She was running with another horse, a big piebald, probably a cold-blood, judging by her feathers." Ryan gestured in the direction of his mount's hooves. "And the piebald was quite wild."

A tingling sensation danced down Sam's forearms. She realized she was clutching one of her saddle strings as if it was the only thing keeping her from falling to her knees. She was getting a bad feeling from Ryan's description, but she had to be sure.

"Piebald?" she asked.

Absorbed by Ryan's story, Jen whisked Sam's question aside with a wave of her hand and muttered, "Pinto or paint, you know."

Sam's fingers went numb as she held on even tighter.

"Until two weeks ago, they stayed together. Chums, you know, and then one day, I rode up here to find she hadn't eaten all the feed I'd left. And she was alone."

As Ryan went on, Sam felt dizzy.

Golden Rose had been running with the big paint mare who'd become the Phantom's lead mare. Or had she?

The timing was right, but a lead mare was skilled at managing the herd.

Sam shook her head. Whatever her status in the Phantom's band, the danger remained. In all the months she'd been watching mustangs, Sam had only seen one free-roaming pinto mare with feathers like a draft horse.

And that mare was dead.

Sam kept her fears to herself as she and Jen rode toward home.

Even though she'd told Jen about the dead mustang, she'd been too concerned with her excitement over Golden Rose to do more than say it was too bad. Sam didn't want to crush her friend's excitement, or worry her unnecessarily. Tonight, Brynna might tell her how the big paint had died. If it was something contagious, then it would be soon enough to tell Jen.

When Jen twisted in her saddle to look back over

her shoulder for about the hundredth time, Sam couldn't helping looking, too. Ryan had told them that Golden Rose usually returned to Nugget at sundown, for her dinner.

*My father rarely tracks my comings and goings*, he'd said, *So I'll wait for her and make sure the bars are up on the stall, so that you can return tomorrow. If you like, I'll try to help you halter her and lead her home.*

As if she could read Sam's thoughts, Jen said, "Ryan's being pretty nice about this, under the circumstances."

Sam couldn't believe Jen's generosity. "Under the circumstances, I think *you're* being pretty nice. Your family has been searching for that horse and he's kept her from you. Whether he knew she was yours or not, he's a horseman, Jen. He had to know she belonged to someone."

Jen shrugged. "How could he tell? Are you positive you could?"

When Jen put it that way, Sam couldn't swear she'd be able to tell. But she still didn't trust Ryan.

"You have to admit the whole thing is pretty weird," Sam insisted.

Jen's mouth curved in a sad sort of smile. "You know what I think? He's been his mother's perfect little English gentleman for years. Now, he's in the Wild West. So, he did something kind of naughty, and he got caught."

What Jen said was possible, but Sam didn't agree.

Ears flicking sideways toward Lost Canyon, Ace shied. Inadvertently, Sam's legs tightened and Ace lunged forward. Silly joined him, and for a couple seconds, the horses moved with choppy, irregular strides.

Both Jen and Sam looked around. In this place of mirages and lost horses, anything was possible. Suddenly, they saw what the horses had sensed.

Hooves rang like slaps against the playa, as two horses exploded out of Lost Canyon. Cream and dusty brick-colored in the dusky light, they might have been primitive figures daubed on cave walls.

"It's her!" Jen gasped.

"With the Phantom."

At first, Sam thought the stallion was driving the mare ruthlessly. His ears lay flat against his lowered head as he sped after her. But then the golden mare gave a playful buck. With ears pricked forward, she ran around a black boulder. Legs leaning in imitation of hers, the Phantom followed. Speed building, their legs slid to the side, but they weren't falling, just taking their zigzag patterns in another direction.

Suddenly, the palomino stopped. So did the Phantom, keeping a few yards between then. Both horses were breathing hard. Their ribs worked in and out as they watched each other.

Tail fanned, knees lifting, the mare pranced a few steps away, then turned her head to look back at him. With a snort, she stopped again, posed, and caught her breath.

The stallion struck out a slim, silver foreleg, then stood waiting for the palomino's next move.

She swished her tail and neighed, daring him to follow, giving him a head start before she took a single step.

Ears flat, eyes forward, he was after her. His mane and tail streamed like white silk.

The mare lunged up and over, hurdling nothing but air. She touched down to the desert floor in a clatter. Her back flattened until it seemed her belly must be skimming the white alkali dust as she galloped back toward Nugget.

They'd given no sign they saw the riders. For them, civilization didn't exist.

"Wow," Sam breathed.

Once the horses were just a blur in the distance, she turned toward Jen. Her friend wore a strained smile. Sam thought she knew why. Jen wanted the mare and so, it appeared, did the Phantom.

"I hope she's having a good time," Jen said. "But she's not going to be the mate of a wild bronc, even if he is your favorite horse in the world." Jen urged Silly into a jog, then looked at Sam. "I hope that's okay with you."

"It's fine with me," Sam said. She stared toward home through the frame of Ace's ears. "But you might have trouble convincing them."

## Chapter Twelve

Once Jen turned off toward Gold Dust Ranch, Sam's mind was filled with the Phantom. Her wonderful, brave, and beautiful stallion was safe and happy.

Whether Jen liked it or not, that was all that mattered to Sam.

"I *am* worried about the rest of the herd," Sam told Ace as they jogged the last mile to River Bend.

The last time the Phantom had been without a lead mare, he'd taken over all her duties himself. He'd looked ragged and exhausted, but he'd kept his herd safe. So where were they now?

Sam hadn't come up with any ideas by the time she arrived home. And then she saw Brynna, leaning her chin on crossed arms as she watched the horses in the ten-acre pasture. Brynna knew more about mustangs than just about anyone.

At the sound of Ace clopping across the bridge,

Brynna turned. As she did, her red ponytail whirled. In jeans and a bright blue sweatshirt, Brynna should have looked cute, for a stepmother. Instead, she looked troubled.

"I'm glad to see you," Brynna called to Sam.

"You are?" Sam said. She drew rein so that Brynna could fall into step beside Ace.

"Can I talk with you while you rub him down?" Brynna asked.

"Sure," Sam said, though Brynna's tone made her wary. "You can go first."

Brynna's face brightened, but she didn't rush into a conversation.

Inside the barn, she watched as Sam stripped off Ace's tack and gave him a good rubdown, trying to dry his coat completely.

"You could be a Popsicle pony if it gets as cold tonight as it did last night," Sam told Ace.

Though they hadn't crossed much snow, Sam checked Ace's feet for ice balls. While she did, Brynna forked hay for the gelding.

"Thanks," Sam said. "Dad always feeds lots of hay in the winter."

Brynna's sigh moved her whole body. Sam didn't get it. It wasn't as if she'd said something mean.

"Yep," Brynna said. "That's what they need to keep going when it's cold." She leaned the pitchfork against the wall, then rubbed her hands together briskly to warm them. "Do you pack any of that white grease in his hooves when it's snowy?"

"Sure. It's in the tack room if you need it," Sam said, giving Ace a pat.

Brynna's hands perched on her hips and she shook her head. "I guess there's not much you can learn from me."

Sam laughed, then realized Brynna was serious.

"Your gram clearly doesn't need my help with cooking," Brynna began.

"Gram doesn't *need* anyone's help cooking," Sam said. "But that doesn't mean she doesn't want it sometimes."

"And she keeps the books, and Wyatt schedules chores for the hands. . . ."

Sam thought of listing things she did for Gram, like grating cheese and coring apples, but Brynna was still talking. As she did, Sam figured out that Brynna hadn't stayed long at work today. Instead, she'd been hanging around the ranch, trying to figure out where she fit in. And she still hadn't come up with an answer.

"Between them, Grace and Wyatt could run the ranch alone."

"Dallas helps," Sam put in.

Brynna's scowl told her she'd said exactly the wrong thing.

"See?" Brynna demanded. "I'm useless around here."

This was weird. Upside-down kind of weird.

Usually adults built up kids' self-esteem, not the other way around.

"Well, I could use your help figuring out what's going on with the Phantom," Sam said.

"His lead mare, you mean?" Brynna shook her head. "I haven't heard from the lab. It will probably be Monday before I do."

"Not just that. There's this other problem."

"Sam, you don't have to make up things to confide, just because I'm having a little pity party." Brynna gave a melancholy smile. "I'll shake it off in a minute."

Sam wasn't so sure of that. In fact, she'd never really thought about the word *forlorn*, but she was pretty sure that was the expression Brynna was wearing.

"This is something I really want to know," Sam insisted. She had to be careful, though. She wouldn't mention seeing the Phantom today, because that would lead to talking about Rose.

"Okay then," Brynna said, leaning forward just a bit. "Ask away."

"I saw Phantom last night—and not in my dreams," Sam interrupted herself when Brynna raised an eyebrow.

"Then where?" Brynna's tone was definitely parental.

"Don't do this split-personality thing to me," Sam said, laughing. "I don't want you to act like my stepmother right now. May I *please* talk to Brynna the biologist?"

"Don't push it, Sam," Brynna said, but the teasing had obviously lightened her mood.

"Okay. I saw him again, this afternoon, between Lost Canyon and War Drum Flats. Both times, he was without his herd. Why do you suppose that is?"

"The obvious answer is that he's lost his herd to another stallion," Brynna's tone was entirely unconvinced. "But it's winter. Stallions aren't out sparring for harems." Brynna's eyes looked unfocused as she twirled the end of her ponytail, thinking. "Still, the Phantom is sort of a rogue. I don't mean that in a bad way. It's just that the usual rules don't seem to apply to that horse."

Brynna was right. The Phantom wasn't entirely wild, but he certainly wasn't tame. Sam thought of people who had wolf dogs. Their wild and tame natures were always battling for control. Maybe that's how it was for the Phantom.

Would it change anything if she told Brynna about Golden Rose?

Sam rocked back on her boot heels. Jen wouldn't like it. This was Jen's secret. Only she and Ryan knew about it, and though Jen hadn't made her take a vow and sign her name in blood, she knew her friend expected that level of secrecy.

More than anything, Jen wanted to surprise her parents.

As she met Brynna's eyes, Sam realized her step-mother had been studying her.

"He doesn't look like he's been hurt, does he?" Brynna asked, misinterpreting Sam's silence.

"It's not that," Sam said.

She'd bet Brynna wouldn't tell a soul about Golden Rose. She probably wouldn't even confide in Dad if Sam begged her not to. After all, they were building a family relationship, right?

Besides that, Dad wasn't much of a gossip. She couldn't imagine him calling Jed up or moseying into Clara's Diner to chatter about Jen's secret.

"If you're having a private conversation with your-self, that's fine," Brynna said, "but if I can help, I will."

"Let me think a minute more," Sam said.

Sweetheart slung her head over the fence dividing her stall from Ace's. She stretched her muzzle in what she must have known was a vain attempt to reach his new serving of hay. Then she nickered pitifully.

Sam gave Sweetheart more hay, while, mentally, she tried to arrange her words so that she wasn't really telling Jen's secret.

"How long does it take for a domestic horse to become feral?" she asked, finally.

"I guess it would depend on the horse. Age would be a factor, and—"

"No, I mean *legally*," Sam said. "Could a horse that's been running around loose for a couple years still be your horse?"

"Do you mean the Phantom?" Brynna asked incredulously.

"No." Sam's frustration built. Brynna knew darn well she wanted the Phantom to run free forever. "Look, if I tell you something, can you not tell anyone?"

"If it puts you in danger—"

"It's nothing like that. It's not even about me."

"Give it a try," Brynna said, "but I'm not making any promises."

"Jen and I found a horse that's probably the Kenworthys' missing palomino. Her name is Golden Rose and she's been gone for two years."

*Great. Just spill the whole thing,* Sam scolded herself.

"Really." Brynna didn't say it like a question at all.

"Yeah. She's been loose a couple years and I'm wondering if the Kenworthys can still claim her."

"I'll call Jed—" Brynna began.

"No, no, no! That's the worst thing you could do. Jen wants it to be a surprise."

Brynna looked disapproving, but she answered Sam's question just the same. "My best advice would be for her to locate the bill of sale, or registration papers, something with an exact description of the horse. After this long, she'd better be prepared just in case someone contests ownership. For instance if someone"—Brynna didn't name Slocum, but Sam knew it was just the sort of thing he'd do—"talked the sheriff into making an inquiry or tried to claim her."

That sounded sensible, and not too hard.

Since she'd told Brynna everything else, Sam added, "The mare came from Mexico. She's a Moorish palomino and she was supposed to be the cornerstone of their palomino breeding program."

"She sounds valuable, and though I'm not familiar with Mexican horse registries," Brynna admitted, "I wouldn't be surprised if the mare has a lip tattoo or a small breed mark, like a brand."

"She might. I've only seen her from a distance," Sam said, but she wanted to rush into the house and call Jen.

Brynna's hint that Linc Slocum might get in the middle of this worried Sam. Ryan Slocum seemed nice, but Sam still didn't trust him. He'd been riding up to Nugget, caring for Golden Rose. Anyone could tell he'd planned to gentle the mare and keep her.

If Ryan was anything like his sister and father, he'd find an underhanded way to claim Golden Rose. Jen needed to find a document proving the mare was the Kenworthys' property, right now.

"Are you shivering or fidgeting?" Brynna asked.

"It is getting pretty cold," Sam said. "Let's go in."

"Great," Brynna said morosely. "I can hardly wait to watch Grace cook."

Gram's lasagna filled the kitchen with the aroma of oregano and cheese.

Gram pulled the big casserole dish from the oven,

then slipped a square cake pan inside and adjusted the temperature. Next, Sam noticed Gram asked for Brynna's help tossing a green salad. It was a simple, no-talent job. Sam knew this because it was usually hers.

Brynna did it, but she didn't exactly rejoice at Gram's faith in her culinary skills. As they sat eating, Sam felt tension coursing among the adults. They were all so polite, it was creepy.

Sam tore her slice of garlic bread in half, thinking of how she'd asked for Brynna's help out in the barn. She didn't regret it, but what if Brynna took her on as a project?

Sam tore her bread into quarters. If Brynna decided stepmothering was the one thing she could do right around here, she could become a pest.

Wind whistled around the house and the windows shook a little in their frames. It was the next-to-the-last night of winter vacation and the truth was, she wouldn't mind spending it anywhere but here.

Sam thought it might not be so bad sleeping in the barn with Ace. Curling up in that deep straw would be cozy. She'd read that in the old days, sheiks let their children sleep in their tents with their heads pillowed on the bellies of their Arabian warhorses.

She thought of Ace and smiled. If he wasn't a restless sleeper—

"You want to do what?" Dad asked suddenly.

Sam jumped. She hadn't mumbled something

aloud, had she? Then she realized Dad was talking to Brynna.

Brynna was pretending she'd said something normal, but Sam didn't think so. Not when Gram was giving lots of thought to rearranging her silverware and Dad was holding his pasta-loaded fork in midair.

"I'm good at polishing boots," Brynna said, taking a sip of her milk. "I offered to polish yours. What's the big deal?"

Brynna's voice held steady, but when she looked up, her blue eyes were bloodshot and confused. Dad noticed as soon as Sam did.

"Why don't you take the night off, instead," he suggested. "Go upstairs and take a bubble bath or something."

Sam's spine flattened against the back of her chair. Never had Dad made such a suggestion. As far as she knew, Dad had never even heard of bubble baths.

"I wish you'd tell *me* to—" Sam started and finished in the same breath. Dad's glare said the only bubble bath she was going to get was from the elbows down, when she did the dishes.

It was a great offer, so why was Brynna pushing back from the table, rising slowly, moving in absolute slow motion?

Sam's stomach sucked in. She didn't like the feel of this evening. Not one bit. It was a relief when Dad and Brynna excused themselves to go upstairs.

They didn't make it that far, though.

Even though they were in the other room and Sam and Gram remained at the dinner table, their conversation was loud enough to hear.

"Around here, there's nothing you need me for. I can't do anything useful," she began.

"Not true, B.," Dad said gently. "I just don't think you can do *everything*. We stay home, and you go to work at Willow Springs. You're doing your part. A part no one else can do and we don't want you to change."

As it grew quiet in the living room, a cascade of questions tumbled through Sam's mind. When had Dad started calling Brynna "B."? Had he ever sounded so gentle and supportive before? Should she tell Brynna that *she* certainly didn't want her to change?

Sam jumped when Gram reached over to touch her arm.

"Something for you to remember, Samantha Anne, when you get married," Gram said quietly. "Start off in the way you mean to go on."

Do what? Gram didn't explain, but as she cleared the table, Sam decided she understood. Dad wanted his marriage to be based on what was real. Instead of allowing Brynna to be sad with her wrong assumptions, Dad had just flat-out told her they all liked her the way she was.

Sam watched Gram stir together powdered sugar

and milk in a pottery mixing bowl. Next, she added vanilla flavoring to a frosting for the cake she'd slipped into the oven. As she watched, Sam decided she'd be smart to second Dad's compliments to Brynna. If her new stepmother felt good about herself, it might even keep her out of Sam's bedroom.

One of the few good things about the house's only telephone being in the kitchen was that Sam could wash dishes as she talked with Jen.

Gram went outside to blanket Sweetheart and Sam had the kitchen to herself. By the time she'd finished the dinner plates, she'd told Jen everything Brynna had said about validating the identity of Golden Rose.

"He might try to claim the horse for himself," Sam told Jen.

"Oh, Sam, you're getting as paranoid as I am. He's got his choice of, like, thirty-eight horses on this ranch. You know he's not going to do that."

"I *don't* know that," Sam said, but she didn't add that Jen only thought she did because of her crush on him.

"In any case, Brynna's right," Jen agreed, then her voice dropped to a whisper. "I know where to look for that stuff, but I'm going to need some help."

"What kind of help?" Sam asked suspiciously. She kept her voice down, because she heard Gram's steps on the front porch.

"Tomorrow when you come over, I want you to distract my mom, while I get in this drawer where they keep important documents."

"Why do I have to distract her?" Sam asked quietly.

"Because, as I've said about a million times, I want this to be a surprise." Jen pronounced the last few words carefully, as if Sam was a little slow. Then, Jen's tone turned chipper. "C'mon, be a buddy. Just do it."

Sam pulled the stopper from the kitchen sink. The suds spun into a vortex that sucked them down the drain.

"I'll do it," Sam said, finally. "But I've got a bad feeling about this."

"About what, dear?" Gram said as she came back inside.

"Yeah," said a second, deeper voice. "About what?"

## Chapter Thirteen

Sam hung up the phone and turned to face Gram and Jake, with what she hoped wasn't a phony smile.

"About the other kids in my small group in history," she said quickly. She dried her hands, then went over to her seat at the table and plopped down. "Some of them are real slackers."

Jake gave a short laugh. He wasn't fooled one bit, but Gram just smiled.

"I'll leave you to your studies," she said, "but when the timer goes off for that cake, could you either call me or slap some of that icing on while it's still hot?"

"Sure," Sam said.

Jake stayed next to the front door until Gram had left the kitchen for the living room. Absently, as if he were thinking of something else, he rubbed his leg where it had been broken.

When he noticed her watching, Jake dropped his

backpack to the floor, walked to a chair, turned it around, and straddled it so he was facing her.

"What was Ryan doing out there?" he asked.

It was the last thing she'd expected.

"Why do you care?" she asked.

"Are you protecting him?"

"From what? You?"

His mouth opened in what looked like the start of a snarl, then he looked down at his hands, refusing to take the bait.

"Why are you trying to get me off the subject? Do you like him or something?"

"Me?" Sam knew her screech carried into the other room, but she didn't care. "The day I like a Slocum, you can—" She tried to think of a suitable punishment for being so dumb. "You can have me locked up in a home for the criminally stupid."

"So, what was he doing out there?" Jake insisted.

"Ask Jen, she's the one with the crush on him," Sam said.

That stopped Jake. He even looked surprised.

Though Sam felt ashamed for tossing her best friend out there to lead Jake off the track, she knew Jen would prefer that over telling him the truth.

Jake's surprise passed as quickly as Sam's instant of guilt. His arms hung over the chair back and his eyelids drooped in why-should-I-care laziness.

"I saw your horse," he said then.

There was no question in Sam's mind. Jake didn't

mean Ace. He meant the Phantom.

"Where did you see him? When?"

This time Jake didn't tease her. "Sniffing around Aspen Creek yesterday."

Aspen Creek was only a few miles away. If you rode along the ridge behind River Bend Ranch and Three Ponies Ranch, then went downhill and north-west, you'd come to the spot.

Sam couldn't think of Aspen Creek without pic-turing Moon, the Phantom's night-black son. After his sire had banished him from the herd, Moon had lived along Aspen Creek, sharing his territory with a variety of companions—a cougar, a Shetland pony, and finally a fleet mare he'd stolen from the Phantom's herd.

"Was he alone?" Sam asked.

Jake nodded.

"I saw him yesterday on War Drum Flats," Sam said. "Why do you think he's alone?"

"Could be he came back after the lead mare," Jake said, giving a faint nod toward his home ranch.

"Or . . . ?" Sam encouraged him. Jake had the best horse sense of anyone she knew.

"Or he's on the prowl for another one." Jake shrugged. "Maybe there's some physical barrier between him and his herd. I'm not gonna guess." Then, when Sam didn't nag him to speculate, he said, "You want to take him home, see if his herd's waiting for him?"

It was exactly what she wanted to do. Sam stared at the kitchen clock. She'd bet that she and the stallion could find each other, right now, in the dark. Then she and Jake could lead him home. But if the stallion wanted to go home, he'd be there. Something was keeping him here.

Besides, she'd vowed never to reveal the way to the stallion's secret valley.

"I don't know why you're so stubborn about this," Jake said. His attention wandered to Gram's pantry as Cougar came mincing out, sat, and cleaned a paw while he watched them.

"I'm not stubborn," Sam protested.

Jake rubbed the back of his neck with one hand. Then, for no reason Sam could see, he pulled off the leather string tying back his black hair.

For a minute he dangled the string for Cougar. The kitten pounced, missed, then lost interest. Jake narrowed his eyes at the kitten he'd given Sam, as if it had betrayed him. He caught his hair back, wound the leather tie round and round, then retied it with a jerk.

"I don't mean to hurt your feelings," Sam said.

She could hear Cougar padding around under the kitchen table. Then he plopped his tiny body over the toe of her right boot.

"That's the last thing you should worry about, Brat." Jake looked at her as if she were a child. "You want to keep your big secret? Fine. But don't fool yourself that I can't find his hideout. I saw your goofy look when you came staggering down from the trail that comes up from Arroyo Azul. I know where we set him loose to go home. I'd have a pretty good idea where to start trackin'."

"But you're too honorable to do it," Sam said.

This time Jake's eyes didn't look away from hers.

As a little girl, she'd noticed what she called Jake's mustang eyes. Dark brown and full of wild thoughts, she could only guess what he'd been thinking. Even now, she wasn't sure. Was he flattered or frustrated?

Whatever Jake was thinking, the silence had lasted long enough. Sam didn't like it.

"I guess you *could* find him, if you weren't lazy," she said.

Jake agreed, nodding. "Or maybe I don't see the point in it. The horse will either take care of himself or he won't."

That was supposed to make her feel angry, but Sam kept her temper reined in.

"So why did you come over?" she asked. She jiggled her feet nervously, disturbing Cougar.

"Thought you'd want to know I saw him." Jake moved his legs back, as if he'd stand. But he didn't.

"Well, thanks," she said grudgingly.

She glanced at the clock again. It was barely eight o'clock. She could smell cinnamon, nutmeg, and raisins. Gram's spice cake was almost done. Next, she'd get to slather it with lots of sweet, white frosting.

She heard Jake swallow. It wouldn't be polite to send him off without a slice of cake. In fact, it would be pure torture.

But she could make him work for it.

"Since you're here anyway," Sam said, "d'you want to help me with algebra? The cake'll be done in a few minutes."

Even though he couldn't help swinging his gaze toward the oven, Jake gave a loud, reluctant sigh.

"Guess it don't matter now," he said. He looked up to be sure she grimaced at his grammar. "Already squandered half the night on lost causes, might as well throw away the rest of it, too."

Gram insisted that Sam go to church with her in Darton the next morning.

"What about my algebra?" Sam asked. In a way, she was looking for an excuse. It was the last day of vacation. Even though she wasn't looking forward to being Jen's diversion while she searched for the papers on Golden Rose, Sam wanted to be dressed and ready to hop on Ace the instant Dad said she could ride over to the Gold Dust Ranch.

"You had a double dose of algebra yesterday. I'd like your company on the drive, and a little time in church won't do you any harm. Although," Gram said, as Sam headed upstairs to dress, "I have been wondering if all that mumbling you do over your math papers just might be prayer."

After church, Sam rushed upstairs and changed into riding clothes. She was hurrying toward the barn when she saw a note left on the kitchen table. Something told her not to read it, but family law said that every member of the family could be held responsible for information on a note left in the middle of the kitchen table. So she had no choice.

The first half was printed in Dad's light, upright hand. *Sam, take Buff or Strawberry. They need work.* Beneath this, in cursive that had to be Brynna's, Sam read, *Be home by 4 & get organized for Monday. Vacation is over.*

"As if I could forget," Sam grumbled.

She didn't want to take Buff or Strawberry. Buff was sweet, but he was pudgy and slow. Silly would run him into the ground. She'd have to take Strawberry, but what a crummy compromise. Besides having the shaggy hair of a mastodon, Strawberry was cranky, especially with other mares.

Jen had gotten angry with Silly yesterday for threatening Golden Rose. Sam was pretty sure Strawberry would do no better.

On the other hand, Sam was more afraid of what Dad would do if she didn't ride one of the horses he'd told her to, than she was afraid of what Jen would do if she did.

When Ace saw her, he rejoiced with a volley of neighs. When she left the barn without him, he nickered after her as if he were certain she'd be right back. After she'd caught Strawberry, he kept calling.

Nothing startled or irritated Strawberry on the way to the Gold Dust Ranch. The mare's swinging, ground-eating jog reminded Sam why Dad liked to use her on long trail rides.

They reached the Gold Dust in good time, and Strawberry didn't act up as they rode down the long entrance to Slocum's estate, in spite of the unusual sights. She snorted at the small herd of Brahmas left over from Linc Slocum's rodeo scheme and shied when a shaggy herd of Shetland ponies ran along their fence like a gang of ragamuffin children. But that wasn't too bad.

"Good girl." Sam patted the mare's soft neck before dismounting in front of the foreman's house where Jen lived with her parents.

A few years ago, it had been the only house on the property. After the ranch had been sold to Slocum, though, he'd had tons of dirt hauled in and sculpted into a hill, so that his pillared mansion could look down on the rest of the ranch.

As Sam tied Strawberry to a ring on a hitching post in front of Jen's house, she heard hammering. She noticed a ladder then, and looked up and saw Jed Kenworthy, Jen's dad, on the roof.

People always said Jen's dad and hers looked alike, but Sam couldn't see any resemblance. Jed looked so stern, he was scary.

Just now, he lay belly down on the slant of the roof. He wore a tool belt, but no coat.

Sam shivered in sympathy. Last week, there'd been a terrific sleet storm and she seemed to remember something about the foreman's house roof leaking.

"Hi, Mr. Kenworthy," Sam shouted in his direction.

Jed gave no sign he heard, but working up in the wind, balanced the way he was, couldn't be easy.

Jen bounded out of the house dressed in jeans and a bright-orange sweatshirt with a tiger on the front.

"For courage," Jen said, patting the tiger.

Although Jen looked the same as usual, Sam felt a kind of frantic energy in her friend's greeting.

*She's staking way too much on this horse*, Sam thought as she struggled loose from Jen's boa constrictor hug. But what could she do about it?

"C'mon," Jen said, towing Sam along by the arm. "But first, I need one more thing. Can I carry the key today?"

Without asking why, Sam pulled the key from her pocket and gave it to Jen.

"The key to my dreams." Jen sighed.

Before they went inside, Sam tried to talk sense to Jen, one last time.

"Ask your dad about the bill of sale. Just tell him you've found the horse. He'd be so happy."

"No way." Jen shook her head so hard, her braids slapped her cheeks. "They've been arguing about money all morning. Then, Dad decided today he had to fix the roof. Roofs don't leak in the city, you know."

"Of course they—oh, I get it," Sam said.

"He's so obsessed with moving, I don't even know why he's up there," Jen whispered. "It's cold and the shingles shatter with practically every nail he hammers into them." Jen looked toward the roof. "But it's supposed to snow again and he, uh, isn't too thrilled about the idea of snowflakes blowing around inside the house."

Sam thought of Dad and Brynna, talking out a misunderstanding before it became a big problem.

"Can't you and your mom sit down with your dad and tell him that no matter what, living here is more important than money?"

"That's easy for you to say," Jen said with a humorless grin. "He won't listen anymore. But I think I can shock him into hearing us when I bring that mare home. Today."

"Okay, then if we could just get Jake," Sam suggested. "He's the best roper—"

"And have him take all the credit? Forget it," Jen snapped. She drew a deep breath. "Now, here's my plan. I tried last night, but the document drawer squeaks, so I had to give up. But today, my mom is cleaning the kitchen cabinets. She's taken all the pots and pans out, they're piled all over the place and she's making an incredible racket. It's just perfect.

"You know where my room is," Jen continued.

Sam pictured it. Off the living room was a single long hall. Jen's parents' bedroom lay to the right and the bathroom on the left. The hall dead-ended into Jen's bedroom.

"The drawer is down low, on the left," Jen continued. "Just before you get to my room. I have to kneel to get it open. Then I have to find the paper. So keep my mom talking for a while, got it?"

The Kenworthys' house usually smelled of wood smoke and cookies, but not today. The odors of furniture polish and cleaning supplies permeated a living room that was abnormally neat. No magazines lay on the coffee table. No coffee cup sat next to Jed's chair. The coat hooks by the front door were empty. It was almost as if Jen's mom had decided a move was inevitable, and she was already getting ready to go.

Lila Kenworthy wore a white sweater tucked into jeans and a red bandanna tied over her hair. Shining aluminum pots were piled on the cold stove while she dusted the inside of an empty cabinet. She glanced over her shoulder, gave Sam a quick wave, and kept working.

"I'm going to go change so we can go to Nugget," Jen shouted.

"Fine," Lila said, but she didn't turn around.

Sam had no idea how she was going to talk with Lila. Actually, it didn't look like it would be necessary. Just the same, she felt better talking.

"The ghost town project is going really well," Sam told Jen's mother. "It's kind of a cool little place. There's an old schoolhouse, a general store, a saloon —"

"I know." Lila's voice had a kind of finality that said she really didn't want to hear any more.

Sam heard a squeak of wood on wood. That had to be the drawer. But Lila's head was almost inside a cabinet.

Steps sounded on the ladder outside. Sam felt her pulse speed up. Just because he was coming down from the roof didn't mean he was coming inside, did it?

"Hurry up, Jen!" Sam shouted in the general direction of the hall.

Lila looked over her shoulder with raised eyebrows.

"Sorry," Sam apologized. "I have to be home kind of early today, and I'm not riding Ace. I'm riding Strawberry, our old roan, and she's cranky. I have no idea how she's going to get along with Silly. . . ." Sam let her voice trail off. Not only was she babbling, she'd heard the front door open. Jed stamped his feet as he came inside.

Oh no. Oh *no*.

Jed didn't turn into the kitchen; he stalked through the living room toward the hall.

"What in the . . . ?" Jed roared.

"Dad, it's no big—" Jen's voice drifted down the hall.

"Lila! Lila, get in here and look at your daughter going through the cash drawer!"

Hands clasped together as she ran, Jen's mother hurried from the kitchen. Sam stayed where she was, listening in helpless horror.

"Dad, no! That's not it, I'm—"

*Tell him, Jen. Tell him. Please tell him.*

Sam recited the words silently, but she didn't dare shout them as she wanted to.

"I'm resigning today," Jed shouted. "Look at what this family's come to!"

"Dad, I was just looking for something." Jen's voice was calm, as if the sudden appearance of her mother had settled her.

"Jed, neither of us is hurting for money. We have what we need." Lila's voice lowered to a hiss as she said, "Maybe it's all in your head."

"Maybe I'm sick of living under Slocum's thumb!"

"Fine." Lila sounded almost relieved. "Then say that. Don't say you're doing it for us, because we love our life here."

Jed came pounding back through the house, ignoring his wife's pleas. He glanced toward Sam with a cold fury that told her she'd better follow him out.

He opened the door, then called back over his shoulder.

"You're not going anywhere, Jennifer."

"But Dad, I didn't do anything."

"You caused this whole mess!"

"I didn't!" Jen's voice was heartbroken, and Sam felt the injustice of Jed Kenworthy's punishment as if it were her own.

He slammed the door.

"Mom? I didn't cause it, did I?" Jen asked.

"No, of course not. But you'd still better stay," Lila said, wearily.

"But I can't. I *can't*!"

"Of course you can. Sam will finish up for you."

Sam's heart leaped up. She could get Jake to help. He could track down the palomino. They could bring her back here and maybe, just maybe Jen was right. Maybe Jed's anger would melt when he saw the golden mare.

"Sam, don't do it," Jen cautioned. "Don't do my part. Do you understand me?"

"But I could," Sam began, and then Jen was standing right in front of her.

Tears ran from beneath her glasses and her face was flushed, but Jen was just as determined as she'd been all along.

"Don't do my part."

"Okay," Sam said. "I think I'd better go, though."

"I don't blame you," Jen said.

"Jennifer," Lila said in a cautioning tone.

"I don't. I wish I could go, too," Jen's voice broke

into sobs and she ran into her room and slammed the door.

Sam couldn't wait to get outside, but Lila was walking toward her.

"I'm so sorry, Samantha," Lila said.

As she walked Sam to the door, Lila took a quick look around the living room and Sam remembered how Brynna's wedding dress had been cut and pinned in this room.

With a sad smile, it looked as if Lila was remembering the same thing.

"It's loud, but not hopeless," Lila said. "Believe it or not, Jed is coming around. But what on earth *was* Jen looking for in there, I wonder."

Sam felt hot with guilt, but since Lila hadn't asked her a direct question and since Jen was certainly listening, Sam just shrugged and slipped outside.

Jed was up the ladder, pounding harder than before as Sam mounted Strawberry and rode away.

## Chapter Fourteen

Sam and Strawberry left the Gold Dust Ranch at a gallop. After two or three minutes, Sam couldn't stand the bite of freezing air rushing through her lungs. Then she realized she had nothing to run away from. She slowed Strawberry to a lope, a jog, and then eased her down to a walk.

It was about time to decide where she was going, anyway.

"Whoa, girl," Sam said. She held Strawberry at a stop while she opened her saddlebag and pulled out the wool gloves she'd used to protect the glass lens of her flashlight. It was a tricky operation, donning gloves when her horse wanted to head for home, but it was worth it. "Oh, better. Much better."

If she kept Strawberry headed in this direction, she'd reach Nugget in twenty minutes or so. But the only thing left to do in Nugget—since Jen wouldn't accept her help with Golden Rose—was draw the map. And she didn't need to return to Nugget for that. She already had a rough sketch of the town and details showing where she'd found the artifact.

She could draw a polished version of the map tonight, at home, after she'd reassembled the newspaper article as much as possible. If she let Strawberry have her way, they'd be home in minutes and she could finish off her homework before sundown.

That's what she should do. And it's what she would have done if the Phantom hadn't come to her for help.

Sam looked at her watch. It was just a few minutes after noon. She wasn't expected home until four o'clock.

She could ride into Lost Canyon. That's where he and the palomino had come from yesterday, after all. But she wouldn't explore the canyon. She'd take the zigzag path down to Arroyo Azul and ride along the sand spit until she found the passageway through the mountains to the Phantom's secret valley.

School resumed tomorrow. Classes certainly cut into her riding time.

Yep, she should go. Right now. But she didn't.

There were lots of logical reasons she should ride into Lost Canyon, and only one cowardly reason she shouldn't. The last time she'd been there, a mountain lion had tried to kill her.

But the lion was gone. And she wasn't a coward.

Sam turned Strawberry toward Lost Canyon.

The mare showed her disagreement by giving a snort and pulling against the reins.

Strawberry remembered. On the day of the attack, she'd been riding Strawberry.

"All the same, we're not going home just yet, girl."

With stiff steps and tossing head, Strawberry kept arguing.

Could the mare remember exactly what had spooked her? Or was Strawberry simply responding to her rider's nerves?

Sam exhaled. She made her leg muscles relax and flexed her wrists, one at a time.

"I'm sympathetic," Sam said to the mare. "But I'm not taking no for an answer. I'm in the saddle, so I get to decide. And I decide giddyup." She clucked and grudgingly, Strawberry broke into a jog.

But not for long.

The canyon was literally freezing cold and Sam had to slow Strawberry to keep her from slipping. As they walked, Sam searched for the Phantom. She listened, but she also realized she was reaching out to him in some silent, seeking way that had nothing to do with normal senses.

He wasn't there. She just knew she wouldn't see the stallion in the cold and shadowed Lost Valley.

Strawberry was hyperalert, too, but not as if she sensed other horses.

She was scared. Her head swiveled from side to side, ears pricked forward to catch the slightest sound. Her nostrils flared, testing every gulp of air for danger.

"Everything's fine, girl," Sam told her. "We'll be out of here soon."

Even though the Phantom wasn't here, Sam had to go to his secret valley. She wanted to check on the herd.

Evidence of the cold was everywhere. Where Dark Sunshine had lapped water seeping from a crack in a rock wall, there was a sheen of ice. Snow clumped on the edges of the path where she and Jake had faced down an armed wild horse rustler. Sam tried to sort through memories other than those of the cougar.

When she looked over the edge into the canyon yawning on her left, she didn't take time to admire the sandstone shelves. In autumn, the canyon had reminded her of an amphitheater. Now she only searched for the path down to the river.

There it was.

Deer hooves, with graceful, inward-curving tips, had stamped through the snow into the dark sand underneath.

"Just walk where they did," Sam told Strawberry.

Strawberry set her hooves on the path and slowly angled downward. When the steep descent made the mare go faster down the rock-strewn trail, Sam kept her reins snug. If she lost contact with Strawberry's mouth, the mare would bolt into a gallop and they'd both be in trouble.

*I wish we could run*, Sam thought, then concentrated on breathing evenly.

The pounce had come from behind. Sam remembered the wet leather smell of the cat and rotting meat stench of his breath as he'd knocked her off Strawberry.

The young cougar was gone, though. He'd been transported to another canyon. She had nothing to fear, but it helped to study the floor of the canyon as it drew nearer.

The water in the bottom of Arroyo Azul looked like a single slash of blue ink. The thought had barely crossed her mind when Strawberry overreached. In a heartbeat, metal horseshoes and icy rocks combined to make her slip.

Strawberry neighed wildly, yanking her head to the right. She wanted to circle. She wanted to make sure no cat lurked just behind, planting his paw prints inside those cut by her hooves.

"It's okay, girl," Sam told the mare. "We're all right."

But all Sam could think was: *We almost weren't. We nearly fell. And no one knows where we are.*

Once they reached level ground, Sam let Strawberry drink. Three times, the roan took quick sips, then raised her head, but finally, she blew through her lips and Sam felt the mare loosen beneath her.

When she thought Strawberry was ready for another challenging experience, she opened her saddlebags and touched her flashlight. She wanted both hands free to handle Strawberry, but she wanted to know exactly where to reach for the flashlight in case she needed it.

As she rode the mare up the riverbed, she decided to see how Strawberry did in the darkness. She might do better. Didn't you blindfold a horse to lead it out of a fire? If the horse couldn't see something scary, maybe it wouldn't panic.

At last they reached the tunnel. Sam blinked in the darkness, trying to focus even though she knew she couldn't. Strawberry was cooperative and confident as she moved through the blackness.

Out of the wind, with tons of rock all around, it was warmer. Sam tried to be glad of the improved temperature, but she could never completely push away a fear of earthquakes.

And then the tunnel narrowed around them. Sam leaned closer to Strawberry's neck, chin resting on the coarse mane. The mare lowered her head as the rock roof slanted down, but no matter how close Sam clung to Strawberry, the rock scrubbed the back of her jacket.

Strawberry was at least a hand taller than Ace, and the difference meant a tighter fit, but something else was wrong. Every other time she'd come through here, cracks in the roof overhead had let in daylight or moonlight. Maybe she wasn't far enough along yet, not close enough to the stallion's hidden valley.

She'd only ridden through this leg of the tunnel once before, and then she'd been carried by the Phantom. Not Ace. Sam drew a breath. Strawberry and the Phantom were about the same height. Had she just not noticed the discomfort when she'd been riding the Phantom?

Shouldn't she be reaching the valley by now? Or at least the opening that came out closest to the ranch?

She had to use the flashlight.

"Easy girl. It's going to get brighter in here." Sam winced as she said it. If Strawberry decided to act up, she could batter them both against the stone walls. They'd be injured for sure, and maybe worse.

Shielding the beam with her hand, Sam aimed it overhead. It took her a few seconds to process what she was seeing. The cracks were there all right, but they weren't letting in light, because they were packed with snow.

"Oh no," Sam said, and though Strawberry gave an answering snort, she stood still.

Snow. What if the Phantom couldn't get to his herd because the entrance to the valley was packed with snow? What if there'd been an avalanche? Was it possible or was her imagination running away with her like the wildest, craziest horse?

"I'm going to trust you, girl," she told the mare.

"I'm just going to shine it a little bit ahead of us. Good. Now a little more."

Strawberry stamped once, but she didn't panic.

Sam almost did.

Dead ahead—she couldn't tell how far, exactly, but less than a quarter mile, for sure—the tunnel stopped at a wall of white.

Sam swallowed. Her imagination had been right. She clicked the flashlight switch off.

Strawberry gave a low nicker. As the sound echoed back, she neighed again.

Sam wanted to cover her ears, but there was no room.

Strawberry turned her head to the right. She curved her neck hard, harder, and squealed. She tried turning to the left. Still there was no room.

Strawberry's hooves stuttered in place. Just as she had in the canyon, the mare wanted to circle, to check that nothing scary was behind her. But she couldn't.

Even with the saddle between them, Sam felt the mare's back hump up.

"Don't buck." Sam crooned it in a singsong voice. "Don't buck, pretty Strawberry. I'll get us out of here," Sam promised. "As soon as I figure out how."

## Chapter Fifteen

Strawberry was a cow pony, used to backing against the tension of a rope with a calf at the other end, as cowboys branded or doctored it. But could she back all the way down this tunnel until she reached Arroyo Azul?

"We really don't have much of a choice," Sam said to the mare, and somehow, the realization made Sam feel better. "Back," Sam said, and she used the faintest pressure on the bit.

Strawberry gave a confused snort.

*You want me to back up in here?* the sound seemed to say. But Strawberry took a step backward.

Sam dropped her reins against the mare's neck, rewarding her. "Good girl, very good girl."

Once more, with the slightest finger pressure, Sam tightened her reins and clicked her tongue. Strawberry backed again. Sam lowered the reins.

Strawberry knew what she wanted, now. Did she

dare give her the order to keep backing?

Sam lifted her reins and clucked and Strawberry moved back. Cluck, step, release. Soon Strawberry was moving automatically and the tunnel was brightening around them. At last, they were out.

Sam closed her eyes and hugged Strawberry.

Backing was hard, making the horse move her hind end up under herself. She might be sore tomorrow, but just now, Strawberry was glad to be out and so was Sam.

It took half the time to ride out of Lost Canyon.

Sam's mind was spinning the whole while. That's why the Phantom wasn't with his herd. He couldn't get back to them. He was snowed out.

How could she help?

When River Bend came into sight, Sam glanced at her watch and smiled. It was only three thirty. So much for Brynna's underlined four o'clock. She was actually home early. She had all afternoon to do her homework and figure out how she could reunite the Phantom with his herd.

Only Blaze came out to greet her.

Sam swung down from the saddle and rumpled the Border collie's ears. He licked her hand, ran a lap around her and the horse, then returned to the front porch to resume his afternoon nap.

Gram had driven over to Mrs. Allen's house, Sam remembered. Dad and Brynna were probably inside, enjoying a lazy afternoon alone.

Sam took her time tending to Strawberry. She brushed the mare with extra care, hoping the muscle massage would keep her from tightening up. When she was ready to release her, Strawberry gave Sam a whiskery nibble on the neck, then trotted off to join the others.

Sam crossed the yard to the house and slipped into the kitchen. The whole house stood quiet, so she didn't slam the door or call out.

She opened the refrigerator and was staring inside when Dad's voice came to her from upstairs.

"One of the first things I noticed about you was that open, free look. No one could tell you what to do."

"I know," came Brynna's voice.

"I love you, and this is your home," said Dad.

Glad as she was that Dad and Brynna's marriage was off to a good start, Sam decided she should close the door between the kitchen and the living room, so she didn't overhear any more of their lovey-dovey conversation.

She'd just moved the doorstop and started to ease the door closed when she heard her name.

"Sam's your daughter, though. Is it right for me to say something?"

Dad's voice rumbled an answer, but it was too quiet for Sam to hear the words.

"I'm concerned. At worst, she's somewhere she shouldn't be. At best, she hasn't told us the truth.

Wyatt, I won't be lied to," Brynna said.

*Uh-oh.*

What were they talking about?

Suddenly her appetite vanished and she decided she should get this over with now.

"Hi, I'm home," she called up the stairs.

"Sam, could you come up here?" Dad said.

Sam glanced into the living room mirror. She looked messy and dirty. Yikes, how had her face gotten all smudged? Had she rubbed it on the side of the tunnel?

Using her fingers, she tamed her auburn hair into a disheveled curve. It looked better. More windblown than scruffy.

"Sam?" Dad's voice was louder.

"Coming!"

Okay, Sam thought as she climbed the stairs. It couldn't be that bad. All the really major family confrontations took place around the kitchen table.

They stood together in the hall between her room and theirs. Brynna's arms were crossed and Dad stood right behind her, close enough that their shoulders touched.

"This doesn't look good," Sam joked.

"Where have you been?" Brynna asked.

She didn't sound angry. It wasn't like she was demanding to know, but the question was clearly a trap.

"Well, I went over to Jen's," Sam began. "You

told me I could, and your note said I didn't have to be home until four. I've been out taking care of Strawberry since three thirty and I just came in and was looking for something to eat because I know Gram's not going to be home for"—Sam heard her nervous chatter—"a little while."

Brynna looked up at Dad. "Does she always babble when she's in trouble, or is it just me?"

"Always has, probably always will," Dad said.

Now Sam crossed her arms. She didn't want to start an even bigger conflict, but she didn't want them making fun of her, either. And she really didn't like the word "babble."

"Jen called here looking for you," Brynna said.

"When?" Sam asked cautiously.

No one said anything. The longer they were quiet, the more convinced Sam was that Jen had called right after she'd left. Hours ago.

"You said I didn't have to be home until four," Sam repeated.

"And you said you'd always let us know where you were," Dad said.

"Keeping that information to yourself and letting us believe you were just over at the Kenworthys' is a lot like lying," Brynna added.

"You're ganging up on me," Sam said.

"You can look at it that way if you like," Dad said, shrugging. "But that's how things are going to be from now on. Except when your gram's involved."

"Then we'll work as a team," Brynna said.

"I don't think this is funny!" Sam snapped.

"Neither do we, young lady."

Oh boy. When Dad got to the *young lady* stage, she was really in trouble.

"But I didn't lie," she said meekly. "What's my punishment?"

"Your dad says Blackbeard's Closet could use a good cleaning," Brynna mused.

"Not that, please," Sam said. She folded her hands together and let them dangle demurely in front of her.

"We haven't decided for sure yet," Brynna said. "It will depend on your behavior over the next few days. And the grade you get in math."

"You're just going to hold the punishment over my head?" Sam moaned.

"Yep," Dad said, nodding. "That's pretty much it."

Should she feel relieved or angry?

Until she knew, Sam decided to keep her tangled feelings to herself.

"May I please be excused to my room to do homework?" she asked.

"Go ahead," Dad said, but a look passed from him to Brynna that said something about leaving homework until the last night of a two-week vacation.

Before they could bring that up, too, Sam stepped into her room and gently closed the door.

❖ ❖ ❖

Sam worked hard, using colored pencils and plain white paper from Brynna's computer to sketch out a map of Nugget. While she worked, she thought about the Phantom. He was probably somewhere with Golden Rose.

Even if he was alone, he'd be safe. And, inside the sealed-off valley, the mares and foals were probably safe as well. The valley had water and graze. She imagined the horses pawing through a crust of snow. They might be awfully thin if they couldn't get out before spring.

Before dinner and after, Sam tried to telephone Jen, to see which part of the project she wanted to do, but the busy signal continued for hours.

Finally, at eight o'clock, Sam gave up hope. She wasn't going to reach Jen tonight. By accident or on purpose, the Kenworthys' phone must be off the hook.

Sam sat cross-legged on her bed, looking at the stuff spread before her. She didn't have much choice. She had to buckle down and do it all.

There was one thing she'd been dreading doing, just because she was afraid she'd mess it up — reassembling the delicate old pieces of newspaper.

But that was their artifact. And the artifact had to be handed in with notes explaining what it was.

Sam looked at the clock. Now it was 8:10 and only half her project was done. Her teeth sawed against her lower lip. She'd really wanted Jen to do this part, but it wasn't going to happen.

Sam went to the bathroom for a pair of tweezers and a pure white towel. She spread the towel on her bedroom floor. Next, she used the tweezers to lift out each one of the newspaper fragments and place it alone. Then she searched for edges and ideas that seemed to match.

Once, as she bent over the yellow-brown shards of newspaper, someone peeked in her door.

She'd just found three words that completed an entire paragraph of one of the stories—it turned out she had most of two—and she didn't look up to see who it was.

"Hi," Sam called out, eventually, but when she looked up, whoever had been there wasn't anymore.

Sometime later, she sat back with a sigh. Her right foot was asleep. She shook it, and rolled her shoulders, which felt cramped from the taut position she'd maintained since . . . Sam looked at her clock. It was 10:45.

"Your dad tells me it's way past your bedtime."

Startled, Sam looked up to see Brynna leaning partway in her door. Her stepmother was still dressed, but her pale blue tailored shirt had pulled free of her jeans, more of her hair hung loose around her face than was captured in her braid, and she yawned as she waited for Sam's response.

"You've got to see this," Sam said, suddenly aware

she'd been longing to share this discovery. "It's an old newspaper. The pieces I have don't show a date, but it's really cool."

Brynna took a long step over the white towel to stand behind Sam.

"'Costly Vermin Invade Nugget Town'?" Brynna read a headline aloud.

"Yeah, this one is about rats just attacking the whole place. The store—it's still up there, you know—the saloons, and even the mines. It says—look! See?" Sam pointed. "Cats were being imported and they cost twenty dollars, which was 'more than a solid saddle horse.'"

Brynna sat on a corner of Sam's bed and Sam found she really didn't mind.

"I'm pretty sure I wouldn't like to be down in a dark mine with hungry rats," Brynna said, shuddering.

Chills trickled down Sam's neck and arms as she thought of the midnight-black tunnel she'd been in today. Thank goodness they hadn't encountered any rats. Strawberry really would have gone nuts.

"The only safe place was the school, and they attributed that to"—Sam read the name—"'Miss Marjory Johnson, schoolmistress, and her godly cleanliness.'"

"What's the other one?" Brynna asked.

Sam sighed. She really wished she'd assembled the rat one first and just stopped.

"It's really sad. And it's not all here," Sam said,

"but it explains the little coffins I found in the ice-house."

Brynna caught her breath. "Little coffins?" she repeated.

Sam held her hands about four feet apart, then swallowed hard as she turned back to the newspaper. The headline was the worst part. If she could get past that, she could read the rest of it to Brynna.

"The headline says, 'Oh Our Children!' and then, it goes, 'Six little ones, over half the childish population of Nugget Town, took wing from parents' reluctant arms in a mysterious malady visited upon the scholars of Nugget Town school.'" Sam took a deep breath. She was almost through. "'Among the new angels'—and that's where it ends. It's not broken apart though, it's straight, like someone cut out this first paragraph listing the names."

Finally, Sam risked a look back over her shoulder. Brynna's face was right there, practically touching hers, and Brynna's blue eyes swam with tears for the long-dead children. She touched Sam's shoulder, but her eyes were fixed on the article.

"As if someone cut it out for a keepsake," Brynna said.

Sam nodded.

Brynna cleared her throat and when she spoke again, she sounded like her usual sensible self. "How do you propose to hand that in to Mrs. Ely?"

"I've been trying to figure that out," Sam admitted.

"I kind of think it might be a bad idea to glue it down to paper."

"I'm no historian, but I agree. It might compromise the value of what you've got there." Brynna seemed lost in thought for a minute, then asked, "How early are you willing to get up?"

"For what?" Sam asked, but part of her question was smothered with a yawn.

"There's a photocopy machine in my office. We could take these up to Willow Springs, place each of your little fragments facedown, and—"

"Great idea! Let's go right now!" Sam clapped her hands together. "Why didn't I think of that about two hours ago?"

"You were busy," Brynna said. "And that's okay, because tonight is out. Get this put away and lay out your clothes for tomorrow. Warm clothes, because the temperature is supposed to drop down to six degrees tonight. And I'll wake you at . . ." Brynna gazed at Sam's bedside clock and then shivered. "Five thirty. That ought to give us plenty of time to drive up there and back to your school."

Sam yawned again. "Maybe five forty?"

"You're not going to be late your first day back," Brynna sounded firm, but not impatient.

"Okay," Sam said, already planning to wear the great black sweater Aunt Sue had given her for Christmas. Jen hadn't seen it yet. "But wait. What about Jen? She'll be standing at the bus stop, wondering what happened to me."

"Which do you think she'd rather have, your company or an A project?" Brynna asked.

Sam knew Jen could tolerate a lonely bus ride far easier than a low grade.

"Five thirty," Sam agreed. Then, as Brynna padded down the hall to her room, she called after her. "Thanks! And tomorrow? I'll make you coffee while you warm up the truck."

## Chapter Sixteen

Sam got to school in plenty of time for class. In fact, she was sitting on the freshly buffed linoleum floor outside her locked history classroom, trying to stay awake, when Mrs. Ely arrived.

Sam tried to lift her eyelids, found it to be way too difficult, and tilted her entire head back against the wall instead.

Dressed in a sage-colored wool suit with big brass buttons on the jacket, tiny blond Mrs. Ely looked entirely too energetic.

"I never thought of you as an overachiever, Samantha," she said.

Sam searched for a clever response. First she'd have to decide whether Jake's mother was complimenting or criticizing her. And that task was just too tricky for her sleep-deprived brain.

"Hi," she managed.

Mrs. Ely's keys jingled as she unlocked the

classroom door and stood holding it open. "Up late?" she asked.

"And early," Sam said, pushing to her feet. "I think it's the early part that's messing me up, but wow, wait 'til you see our artifact!"

Mrs. Ely's smile gave Sam a sudden jolt of energy and she bounded into the classroom after her teacher and showed off the copy Brynna had made of the ghost-town newspaper.

Ten minutes later, Mrs. Ely had cleared off a table and arranged the copy, the map, and Sam's notes on top.

"This will give everyone something to shoot for," she said, then gave Sam a pat on the back. "Good work, girl. So far, you and Jen have an A."

Jen wasn't enrolled in Sam's history class, so she didn't expect to see her. But she *was* supposed to be in second period P.E. and when she wasn't, Sam couldn't help worrying.

By lunchtime, she still hadn't seen Jen.

Sipping a chocolate milk shake, which sort of counted as lunch, she spotted Jake.

He wore a jean jacket open over a tee-shirt that matched the buckskin tie holding back his hair. He walked on the fringe of a group of five or six boys. She hated going over there to try to cut him out of his crowd, but she did it anyway.

With slicked-back hair and baggy pants that

threatened to slip to the floor, Jake's friend Darrell noticed Sam first.

"Hey, Samantha you little heartbreaker, that sweater is lookin'—"

"Shut up, Darrell," she snapped. "Jake, I need to talk with you."

For some reason, Jake always looked bigger and broader-shouldered indoors, but it didn't matter. He was her only real friend besides Jen.

She motioned him away from his group. Practically dragging his feet, Jake went.

"Jen's not at school today," Sam said.

Jake leaned against a locker. In spite of the whistles and whoops from his friends, he met Sam's gaze. But he didn't say anything.

"She's not here," Sam repeated.

"Okay," he said.

"Listen, that might be no big deal for some kids. Lots of them are absent the first day back after a break, but Jen is never out on the day a project is due." Sam slammed her hand against a metal locker. "Never!"

Jake looked calm and patient as he considered the locker she'd just pounded.

"Brat, it's January," Jake said. "You've known Jennifer Kenworthy since September. Five months. So, what's with *never*?"

He'd made a good point, but she didn't like it.

Sam shifted her backpack to a more comfortable

position. Her back ached from yesterday's tunnel trauma. She imagined Strawberry was pretty sore, too.

"Okay, you've known Jen longer," she said to Jake. "Do you think this is normal for her?"

Jake darted a look over her shoulder, then he moaned. "I don't know."

"Fine," Sam snapped and walked away, toward her journalism class.

"Glad we got that settled," Jake said to her retreating back.

Sam sighed. For a relatively smart guy, Jake was hopeless. He didn't even know when "fine" meant just the opposite.

The bus ride home was miserable. It was supposed to be a time to go over the high and low points of the day with Jen. Instead, Sam stared out the window, watching the beige landscape slip past.

The walk home would have been endless, worrying about Jen every step, but it was cut short when Gram picked her up.

The yellow Buick was waiting when Sam stepped off the bus.

"I had to run in to Alkali for chicken wire, so I thought I'd give you a lift on my way home," Gram said.

She didn't mention the fact that Jen was missing, and Sam guessed it was because she was so involved in her plan to foil the hungry ground squirrels that had invaded her garden.

"I'm going to lay chicken wire on top of the flowerbed where I planted my tulips, then put mulch on top. I know those squirrels are hungry in winter, but they'll have to find something to munch on besides my tulip bulbs."

Sam was only half listening, but the mention of ground squirrels reminded her of the little corpse she and Jen had spotted next to the stream running down the ravine behind the abandoned schoolhouse.

Sam closed her eyes, but that only allowed the horse skeleton with its dark, empty eyes to make another dancing gallop through her brain.

It was probably stupid to try to make a connection between the plague that had killed those long-ago schoolchildren and the dead squirrel, but she couldn't help trying.

"Did you hear from Brynna about what killed that pinto mare?" Sam asked Gram as the car bumped over River Bend's bridge and into the ranch yard.

"As a matter of fact, I did, dear," Gram said.

Sam's heart pounded as she waited for Gram to go on.

"She said they found signs of arsenic poisoning."

"Like rat poison?"

"No, the naturally occurring sort. It's quite common in mining areas and there's a good deal of it in the water."

Dizzied by the news, Sam closed her eyes. Those

children! All those little coffins had been made for students at the school and the school backed up to the ravine where Jen had found the horse skeletons.

But maybe she was wrong. Golden Rose had been with the paint mare in Nugget and she was alive.

She had to talk with Jen. Now.

Sam shoved open the car door as soon as the Buick came to a stop.

"Gotta call Jen!" Sam shouted. As she bounded for the house, Blaze frolicked around her ankles, barking.

Sam's hands shook as she dialed Jen's number.

"Hello?" the voice was Lila Kenworthy's and she didn't sound a bit concerned.

"Hi, may I please speak to Jen?"

"Sam, she's not home yet. You made awfully good time." Lila paused as if she were glancing at a clock.

Not home yet. It sounded as if Lila thought Jen had taken the bus home. Where was she?

"I got a ride home with my gram," Sam said.

"That explains it. I'm sure she'll be here soon. I'll have her call when she gets in."

"Thanks," Sam said slowly.

Just because Jen wasn't there, didn't mean she was at Nugget. Maybe Jen had a doctor's appointment. Or an adjustment to her glasses prescription. Maybe her mother knew she hadn't gone to school.

"Oh, wait," Lila said, just as Sam started to hang

up. "I'll ask Jen when she walks in the door, but I'm so eager to hear. How did Mrs. Ely like the project you two have been working on?"

Sam tried to think how to answer.

"Mrs. Ely thought it was great," Sam said. "She put it on a table, alone, as an example to everyone else."

After she'd accepted Lila's congratulations, Sam hung up and stared out the kitchen window.

The day had turned bright with winter sun. That was a good thing, because she had a feeling Jen was in a place of death and shadows. She'd need all the sunshine she could get.

Sam whirled through her chores and saddled Ace. Once they were over the bridge, she put the mustang into a lope.

She tried to tamp down her panic. It wasn't like Jen would drink out of that stream. And if she'd taken Silly with her, she'd tie her down on the main street, away from the ravine. And Golden Rose must have a natural immunity. Or maybe she could smell something wrong with the water.

Or maybe the paint mare had found the arsenic water somewhere else entirely.

Sam drew a deep breath. She could feel Ace's uneasiness. It wasn't his fault any of this was happening, so she talked to soothe him.

"You like this wet going, don't you?" she asked

the gelding as they traveled in a balanced, swinging gait. "If you were a racehorse, you'd be a mudder."

Every inch of the week's snow and ice had melted under today's warm sun. The sagebrush was brighter green and the madrone branches up on the hillside were the red of dark chili powder. The earth was soft and spongy, turning to chocolate-colored mud at the touch of Ace's hooves.

Her spirits lifted, hoping the entrance to the Phantom's valley would unseal itself. She pictured the wall of snow at the end of the tunnel melting, and foals playing in the resulting mud puddle.

And then she thought of the Phantom with Golden Rose. She wouldn't take him back to the ravine, would she? If he drank there . . .

All at once, Ace flung his head higher. His lope stayed smooth, but he swerved to one side. And then Sam saw the rider, too.

She recognized Ryan Slocum on the brown Thoroughbred named Sky. They were covering ground in an effortless run, coming straight at her.

Ace lifted his forefeet from the ground in excitement.

"Not you, too," Sam scolded him. "Only Jen has permission to be ridiculous over Ryan Slocum."

They'd probably caught the mare together, Sam thought. They'd probably haltered her, led her around for a few minutes, then popped a saddle on her. Jen was probably getting ready to ride her home.

And they'd done it all without her.

Sam's imagination ground to a halt when she saw Ryan. He wore a close-fitting black leather jacket zipped closed over an oatmeal-colored sweater. He looked like a sophisticated model for an equestrian catalog. He also looked frantic.

"Can you possibly talk sense to Jennifer, because I've failed miserably, and I think she could actually be in danger."

"Why?" Sam could barely get the breath to make the word audible.

"She's fencing off the ravine. She has some sort of entrenching tool—one of those little collapsible shovels—and she's fenced off the low end of the ravine to form a trap."

"She doesn't know how to do that," Sam said. And she shouldn't, Sam thought. If she penned the mare in with only a contaminated stream for water, she'd kill her.

"A point that's escaped her, but which is obvious to anyone observing the blood on her hands." Ryan's lips pressed together in a firm line. His voice stayed level as he added, "I tried to talk her into accepting my help, but she refused."

In spite of Ryan's agitation, he stayed in control of his voice, his body, and his horse. Sky stood quiet. He bobbed his head at Ace's friendly nicker, then returned to statue stillness, wearing the focused look of a horse awaiting his rider's instructions.

"Why doesn't she just lead her home?" Sam wondered.

"A question I asked. After all, I wasn't holding Rose against her will. I fed and curried her until she forgot why it was she wanted to run away. She may have forgotten where home is, but I believe she's willing to return."

Ryan made sense. Even mustangs could be won over with kindness and dependable meals. It should be much easier with Golden Rose. Generations of her ancestors had known the comfort of stalls.

"Did you tell Jen all that?"

"She wouldn't listen. Her trap is made, so she's waiting for the palomino to return. She's adamant about that."

"If you mean she's being stubborn, you're right. Jen can be the queen of stubborn."

"Normally, such obstinance wouldn't be a problem, but the water running off the hillside, through the ravine, is rushing quite swiftly."

*That's good*, Sam told herself. Standing water would have a higher concentration of arsenic. Snow runoff could dilute it.

"Should I notify her father?" Ryan asked.

"Not yet," Sam said quickly. "Let me try to talk to her first."

But Sam knew it was a last try. She might be riding for help, if Jen stayed stubborn.

"I'll go on then, if you believe you can convince

her." Ryan didn't look as if he wanted to leave Sam to deal with Jen on her own, but it was the right thing to do. Jen wouldn't back down in front of him.

"Of course I can convince her," Sam promised. "I'm her best friend."

But as Sam gathered her reins and rode toward the ghost town, she wasn't really so sure.

When she saw Jen, Sam knew getting her to leave Nugget was a lost cause.

Lightweight fence posts, the shovel, a staple gun, and plastic fencing were scattered around at the low end of the ravine. Jen had made a passable holding pen for Golden Rose, but that wasn't what worried Sam.

It was the other palomino she'd ridden past as she came down Nugget's main street. Champ, Linc Slocum's big gelding, was tethered to the hitching rail. Jen had not only cut school, she'd stolen a horse.

She'd have to be careful the way she handled Jen. She couldn't just blurt out the news about the arsenic, or Jen would be even more determined to stay and catch the mare. Sam shivered, feeling like a hostage negotiator. But Jen was only holding herself hostage.

She left Ace with Champ for company, and started on foot toward the ravine. Jen saw her coming, and met her.

Jen's white-blond hair blew in messy disorder and a smear of blood marked her temple. Before Sam could ask what had happened, though, Jen disentangled a lock of hair from the frames of her glasses and Sam saw the burst blisters on her palms.

Sam sighed. Blood showed on the denim covering Jen's thighs, too, but only because she'd been wiping her hands on them.

Arms crossed in stubborn firmness, Jen stood on the other side of the fence, waiting.

"You giving up a career in veterinary medicine for a life of crime?" Sam called to her. "Suspension from school's not so bad, but I don't know what they do to horse thieves these days."

"They don't hang them," Jen said, and as she gave a weary laugh, Sam thought there might be hope after all.

## Chapter Seventeen

$S$am walked through the schoolhouse garden, stepping carefully until she met Jen at the fence.

"Have you told my parents I cut school?" Jen asked.

Sam sighed in relief as Jen raised a canteen to her lips to drink. She'd brought her own water.

And there were no horses in sight. She could quit worrying about the arsenic.

"No, I didn't tell. And I asked Ryan not to get them all stirred up, but they're bound to be wondering. It'll be dark in another two hours." Sam paused to look back down at the horses. Champ and Ace had shifted to the ends of their reins. They looked restless and alert. "Are you hoping the surprise of Golden Rose will make them forget your, uh, mistakes?"

"Yeah, and I think it will work."

Sam didn't ask how, because it didn't matter.

Jen had to get home. Although the sun still shone,

the temperature had dropped even lower than the predicted six degrees last night. Jen's pink parka wouldn't protect her overnight.

She would freeze to death without shelter, and the town of Nugget would have one more ghost.

"While you've been up here working, did you find any more skeletons?" Sam asked.

Jen's eyes got bigger and she wrapped her arms around herself. "There are all kinds of little bones up here. Rodents and birds, but only two horses. It's not that they scare me, or gross me out," Jen said solemnly. "After all, I am a scientist at heart. But it makes me sad. It's the opposite of what I want this place to be. Don't laugh, but I've been doing a lot of thinking. I want this to be a place for rebirth. You know? I'll catch Golden Rose and my dad can start over with Kenworthy palominos."

They heard the first hoof as Jen screwed the top back on the canteen.

They looked at each other, then up the ravine.

Backlit by afternoon sun, the Phantom and Golden Rose stood together. Her palomino coat shone like flame against the cool silver of his. Their manes flowed to the left, pale and silken. Muscles bunched, they watched the humans.

Sam let her breath out by degrees.

It was the wrong time of year for horses to take mates, but these two were surely friends. Locked off from his family, the Phantom had found Rose. Lonely after the pinto's desertion several weeks ago, she'd joined his tiny herd.

Champ and Ace were neighing now, but only Rose gave a sign that she cared.

"Here they come." Jen breathed the words as the palomino, quiet and graceful as a doe, picked her way through the boulders.

As she drew near, the mare stopped in a narrow place where she was flanked by purplish rock, and the dirt was bare of boulders. Sam noticed the dark sweat patches on her coat. The horses had been running and the mare was headed for water.

"Keep her away," Sam said, but her eyes were on the Phantom.

The stallion snorted and shifted. He had to be as thirsty as Rose, but something kept him from coming to the water. Was it their presence, or did he sense something was wrong?

Rose was only yards away from Jen.

Jen held a coiled rope. "If you mess this up for me, I'll never forgive you," Jen yelled at Sam.

Sam didn't listen. "Get out of here!" she shouted, waving her arms.

The mare only looked quizzical.

With a snort of anger, the stallion came after her.

He leaped to the barren spot between the purple rock walls, then came down at a hoof-hammering speed to slash harsh bites on the mare's rump.

Her squeal echoed along with Jen's shout.

"No!" Jen yelled, as if the bite had hurt her, too.

Floating like a ghost horse, the stallion was already past the length of the mare's body and passing in front of her. He was no more than six feet away from Jen. Standing between her and the palomino, he used his body to sweep the mare back from the water.

"Leave her alone!" Jen shouted, but this time she threw the canteen.

A thud on shoulder muscle. And then there was a clatter of hooves as the Phantom backed from Jen and Rose. For the space of a heartbeat, he looked at Sam.

The stallion's dark brown eyes peered through his shaggy forelock, asking why.

He'd come to her for help, and she'd failed him. Looking at Jen as she raged toward the stallion, Sam wondered which one of them really deserved her friendship.

"Knock it off," Sam yelled at Jen. She gave her a push and the violence of her movement sent the Phantom leaping back up the rocky slope to the top of the ravine.

He was gone by the time Jen recovered enough to gape at her.

"I didn't hurt him!"

"I don't care. You tried." Sam leaned forward. Her nose was almost touching Jen's and she wanted to push her down.

"He was trying to steal Rose."

"No he wasn't," Sam insisted. "He was trying to stop her from drinking. There's arsenic in the water. At least, they found it in the dead pinto. And she was up here. Remember?"

Sam heard her own uncertainty, but it made too much sense to ignore.

Jen held her hands over her eyes. When she uncovered them, Sam couldn't tell if she was laughing or crying.

"Sam, you don't really believe that, do you? He wanted to add her to his harem."

Jen was laughing.

With the Phantom safe, Sam wanted to unleash all her worry and anger on Jen.

Instead, she turned to walk away. But she didn't make it very far.

"I tried to help you every way I could, and it wasn't enough," she shouted over her shoulder. "Good luck with your parents, because I'm out of here."

"Oh, Sam, come back here," Jen called.

But Sam could still hear the laughter in Jen's voice. She'd had enough. She mounted Ace and rode out of the ghost town, leaving Jennifer Kenworthy on her own.

Ace didn't waste any time in distracting Sam from her dark thoughts. The little bay mustang proved he'd had yesterday off. After all the excitement in Nugget, he was ready for a run.

For a while, Sam wondered if the Phantom was nearby. Her eyes scanned every foothill in the distance and every inch of playa unrolling before her.

Finally she decided she couldn't blame the Phantom for Ace's energy. She saw no sign of him. What she did see was three Canada geese walking on the playa.

When they were still a mile away, Ace started trotting sideways, ears cocked in their direction.

"It's weird, but you can handle it," Sam told her horse. "Maybe they were on their way to California and mistook this for the beach."

As they drew closer, Sam realized the majestic birds were actually circling a tuft of pale winter grass.

"Maybe the thaw exposed something they like to eat, Acey," Sam told her horse.

Ace clearly wasn't interested in her Discovery Channel narration. When the geese honked in his direction, Ace started shaking.

Sam reined him away.

"Don't be a baby," Sam told him.

This afternoon was going from bad to worse, and if she got home after dark she couldn't guess what Brynna and Dad would do to her. Yes, she could. She'd be cleaning Blackbeard's Closet.

All at once, the geese began running for takeoff. After a few flat-footed, accelerating steps, they were airborne. Wind rushed through their wings. They flapped. They flew. They rolled shining black eyes as they rose into the sky.

It was too much for Ace and he began to buck.

Sam lost her reins, made a grab for the horn, and missed. Ace twisted out from under her like a sidewinder.

She hit the playa with a thump that knocked the breath out of her. She raised up to see him running, but she couldn't get the oxygen to call him back. Ace was running for home, without her, and all Sam could do was sit there and try to breathe.

There was no sense waiting for him to come back.

Sam stood. The geese were gone, but she saw something on the horizon. A truck was coming her way.

Jed Kenworthy's truck moved in a cloud of vapor and Sam realized it was getting cold already.

Both Jed and Lila sat inside the truck. Lila had the window down as they pulled alongside Sam and braked to a stop.

"Are you all right, Sam? What happened? Ryan told us you might need help up at Nugget. Where's Jen?"

"I'm okay," Sam managed to answer one of the questions.

From across the truck cab, Jed leaned forward. "We saw Ace hightailin' it for home." His brown face looked slightly amused.

"Some geese flew practically up his nose—" she broke off, shaking her head. She was still mad at Jen, but her parents deserved to know what was going on. "Jen's still up in Nugget."

Lila opened the door and scooted closer to her husband so Sam had room to sit. "Hop in," she said. "We're going up there."

Sam didn't protest. It was just too bad if Jen didn't want her parents. She needed them.

They'd only driven for a minute when Jed grumbled, "What kinda idiot stunt is that girl pulling?"

Sam glared at him. She could feel herself do it, and though she didn't do it on purpose, she didn't try to stifle the mean look. Instead, she answered him.

"The kinda idiot stunt she hopes will make you happy."

For a full minute, there was only the sound of the truck rolling across the playa. That kind of rudeness wasn't acceptable at River Bend Ranch. If this got back to Dad, she might want to clean Blackbeard's Closet, because it would be her new home.

"We found Golden Rose," Sam said.

"Impossible," snapped Jed.

"How?" Lila gasped.

"Jen's been trying to catch her and bring her home so that you can start your breeding program again and you won't leave the ranch."

Lila took a long, shuddering breath. Her husband frowned through the windshield.

"Well, I'll be," Jed muttered, but he wasn't talking

about Jen and the palomino.

A sea of glittering water spread across the playa. A lavender building floated upside down amid shimmering ripples. The mirage was back.

While Jen's parents marveled, Sam wondered if Jen's plan was just as unreal as the mirage. At first it had seemed magical that Golden Rose had appeared just in time to rescue the Kenworthys. But nothing had changed.

Nothing except Jen had yelled at her and she'd pushed Jen. Hard. They'd done a pretty good job of fracturing the friendship they'd feared distance would end.

Still looking at the mirage, Jed gave a grunt. "Things aren't always what they seem, I guess."

He kept his left hand on the steering wheel and patted Lila's knee with his right.

"Thought you and Jen would like to go someplace sparkly and new. Thought I was doin' it for you. Turns out I was wrong on both counts." Jed narrowed his eyes. "It'd probably just be all dust when we got there, anyway."

A hush filled the truck cab as they passed Lost Canyon.

The mirage thinned to dancing colors, a dim reflection, and then a haze. It had vanished completely by the time they reached the last stretch of road before Nugget.

Sam blinked. She tried to bring something just

ahead into focus. It wasn't another mirage. At first she thought it was sagebrush. Or maybe a white-faced steer. It was too distant to know for sure.

"The road up to Nugget is a mess, as I recall," Lila said. "I guess we'll have to hike in."

"I don't think so," Sam said, because she'd just figured out that the figure up ahead was Jen. She was riding Champ and leading Golden Rose.

Jed braked to a stop, threw the truck into park, and turned the ignition off.

He'd climbed out of the truck by the time Jen dismounted.

Sam reached for the door handle, but Lila touched her arm and shook her head.

"I think it would be best if we let them work this out in private."

Lila's face was filled with longing. She wanted to jump out of the truck and run to them, too, but she didn't.

Jen looked about ten years old. Her father wasn't much taller, but Jen acted as if he was. When she handed him the lead rope attached to the mare's halter, Jen tilted her head back. Her hair had straggled free of both braids. As her father held the rope and stared at the mare, Jen chewed on her thumbnail.

"This is what's been making her act so strange, then," Lila said to Sam.

"You mean crazy," Sam said, and Lila laughed.

"Really, she's been staking everything on this."

In front of them, as dusk closed in, Jen and her father stood talking.

For the first time in months, Sam realized Jed Kenworthy really did look like her own dad. Maybe it was because he looked happy.

"It might have been a good gamble," Lila said. "If Jed has something of his own to work for, he might see an end to living under Linc Slocum's thumb. It was always a compromise, but lately, he's been seeing it as a life sentence."

In the purple-gray twilight, between two golden horses, Jen and her father hugged.

Lila leaned across Sam and rolled down the window. "Want me to drive home and you two can bring the horses?" she called to her husband.

Jed raised his right hand in an OK sign. He kept the other arm around Jen. But then, as Lila maneuvered herself into the driver's seat, Jen's hands waved, trying to keep them from leaving.

She ran to the truck, reached inside, and grabbed Sam's shoulder.

"Ow! Are you trying to pull me through the window?" Sam said, pretending to be cranky.

"I'm so sorry. I know I didn't hurt the Phantom, but I have been acting"—Jen searched for a way to be honest, yet easy on herself—"eccentric."

"Wrong," Sam said. "I told your mom you were crazy and I'm sticking by that."

"I was," Jen admitted with a sigh. Then her face lit with its usual sarcasm. "Crazy as a dog in a meat market, to quote someone we all know and *don't* admire. But it fits, I'm afraid." Jen looked back over her shoulder at her father and the two palominos. "I only had one goal in mind, and I was a jerk 'til I achieved it. But Sam, it might actually work!"

"It might, but you owe me. Big time," Sam scolded.

"We'll think of something," Jen promised.

"Oh no, I've already thought of something."

"Anything," Jen vowed, then waved as she turned back to her father.

"Get plenty of rest between now and the weekend," Sam shouted after her, "'cause you're going to need your energy."

If punishment came crashing down on her, as it probably would, Sam knew who would help her clean Blackbeard's Closet.

## Chapter Eighteen

When Sam reached River Bend Ranch, she expected to see Ace, saddled and trailing his reins, near the ten-acre pasture. Although the little gelding had taken more than his share of kicks in there, he liked to be near the other horses.

He wasn't there. Sam was saying thanks and good-bye to Jen's mom as she surveyed the ranch yard.

There was Jake's truck, and Jake standing impatiently, with arms folded tight, on the front porch.

"Yeah, yeah," Sam muttered to herself. "I'm late for algebra tutoring."

She didn't care. She had to find Ace.

"Have you seen Ace?" Sam called to Jake. "Did he come in riderless and you put him away or something?"

Jake shook his head, so Sam sprinted toward the barn.

"Dad?" her voice echoed. Her only answer was

the fluttering of pigeons in the rafters.

"Hey, I'm not waitin' all day," Jake shouted, as she walked back in his direction.

"I need your help," Sam said.

"That's why I'm here," he said, with a slight bow. "To help the numerically challenged."

Sam brushed his teasing aside.

"This is serious. Ace dumped me out there about forty min—"

"Again?"

"Jake, I need you to take me out in the truck to look for him." Sam didn't try to hide the fear in her voice.

"He'll come home."

"He should've been here by now. I'm worried. Brynna found out that mare died from arsenic poisoning and we don't know for sure where she picked it up."

A flare of impatience showed on Jake's face.

"Never mind," Sam said, sighing. "I'll see if Gram can take me."

"Don't do that," Jake moaned.

"Do what?"

"Act like I've disappointed you. I hate it." Jake jammed his hand into his pocket to withdraw his keys.

Sam gave him a quick hug. "I'll have to remember that," she chirped. Then, she leaned in the kitchen door and called to her grandmother. "Gram, we'll be back in a little while. Jake's taking me to find Ace. He"—Sam gave Jake a glance that said he'd better not contradict her—"wandered off."

Sam had stepped off the porch and headed for Jake's truck when Gram came to the door, wiping her hands on her apron.

"Not so fast, Samantha. It's algebra time."

"I've got to go, really."

"Sorry. I have my instructions," Gram said, shrugging. "Get back in here. And bring him with you."

"Do you know how much I want to go?" Sam knew she was going to be sorry if she said this, but she couldn't leave Ace out alone. It was nearly dark. "Tell Dad and Brynna I'll clean—" Sam swallowed. She really didn't want to say it. "Blackbeard's Closet this weekend."

"You've got a deal, dear," Gram said. And then she closed the door.

Using Jake's binoculars, it didn't take Sam long to spot Ace. Up on a side hill, pawing at the snow in the shade of a peak of the Calico Mountains, he looked quite content.

"I'll drive up as far as I can," Jake said, "but then you're going to walk for it."

Jake swerved off the road and drove the truck cross-country, over weeds and gulches and ruts studded with rock.

"Fine," Sam said.

"Careful of my hat," Jake cautioned. His hand hovered over his black Stetson that held the space between them on the old truck's bench seat.

"Oh, yeah. Wouldn't want to bump the hat," Sam grumbled. "I was just trying to keep from banging my head against the door."

In fact, she was glad Jake wanted her to hike after Ace alone. The gelding was right by the entrance to the tunnel to the Phantom's valley.

This couldn't have worked out better if she'd actually planned it, Sam thought. She and Strawberry had come in from the opposite end near Arroyo Azul. From here, the travel through darkness was much shorter.

If only Jake didn't watch her every move, she could dart inside and see if the snow had melted during the warm spell.

*Please.* Her head snapped back as Jake scraped the edge of a boulder. *Please.* The truck slewed down a channel in the dirt, probably cut by a flash flood. *Please don't let him watch me*, she begged silently.

Suddenly, Jake pulled on the emergency brake. He reached under the front seat, withdrew a big silver flashlight, and placed it in her lap.

"You're hikin' from here, Brat," he said.

Then he placed his Stetson on his head, leaned back, and pulled it down over his eyes.

Sam opened the truck door and climbed out. But

she knew better than to seem glad that she was going alone.

"Hope I don't break my ankle," Sam said, slamming the truck door. "Hope no cougar eats me."

"Can you suffer more quietly?" Jake grumbled. "I'm tryin' to catch a nap."

Stars had pricked through the black sky overhead, but it was still light enough that Sam could see Ace's outline.

He raised his head and nickered in her direction, probably wondering why she didn't call him to her.

"No," Sam hissed. She glanced back over her shoulder at the truck. "Stay there."

Ace did as he was told, even moving a few steps higher on the hill.

Sam climbed steadily, fighting the uneven footing. She pulled the neck of her sweater up to cover her mouth and nose. The air felt icy as she breathed it.

She stopped for a minute, hands on hips, and stared skyward. It had been a long day, but she had to see if the Phantom's herd was safe. She really hoped Jake had fallen asleep.

When she turned back toward the deer path she'd been following, Ace was gone. Sam flicked on the flashlight and swept the beam across the hillside.

"Everything all right?" Jake's voice floated up from the truck.

"Fine," Sam shouted back. "I can see him."

She couldn't, but she knew where he had gone.

That was almost the same thing.

Before she reached the entrance to the tunnel, she heard movement. It had to be Ace. He'd once been a member of the Phantom's herd. He knew where he was going.

Sam hurried after him.

The tunnel was different on foot. She kept the flashlight beam trained down and she was even able to hurry. The rock floor slanted up and down, closed in and flared out, but it wasn't the tight squeeze it had been when she was mounted.

Something grated in the tunnel ahead of her. She stopped and listened. It had to be Ace.

Was he pawing the tunnel floor? He sounded close.

Sam raised the beam to light the tunnel ahead of her.

Ace's black tail was coming at her.

"Easy boy!" Sam called, putting a hand out in front of her.

Ace stopped backing and gave a confused snort at her patting hand.

"There, boy. It's okay, boy." She clucked to her horse. Hands smoothing along his barrel, she moved past him.

He stood looking after Sam, as if her contortions were something worth watching. She had to be almost there.

If she didn't hurry, Jake would come up after her.

She couldn't let that happen.

Then, she saw what Ace had been doing. The tunnel still wore a collar of snow. It had been pawed away at the bottom, but icicles hung from the top like crystals.

Sam turned off the flashlight, held it close to her leg, and pressed against the side of the tunnel. She peered past the silver shafts of ice that framed her view of the snowy valley.

Most of the mares stood dozing. Their smooth black shapes huddled in cozy groups. She heard idle pawing, as a few horses searched for evening snacks. Here and there, she saw dark humps where mares slept with foals snuggled close to their sides. But she couldn't see the Phantom.

Sam didn't want to disturb the wild horses, but she had to know if the stallion was here.

She heard a low nicker, just as she clicked on the flashlight.

Silver and white as if he were sculpted from the snow and ice, the Phantom greeted her. Sam slid the flashlight switch off again.

Barely daring to breathe, she extended her hand. "Zanzibar," she whispered. "You made it home."

First she felt his whiskers. Then his warm muzzle nudged her hand. Velvet-soft lips moved over the delicate skin on the back of her hand. Then he nibbled at her coat cuff.

Jake's voice came to her from the hillside.

"One more minute and I'm comin' up after you."

She had to go.

For another second, Sam stood with her eyes closed, memorizing the stallion's touch. You couldn't always believe your eyes, but your heart wouldn't steer you wrong, she thought.

Suddenly, Sam gave in to an impulse. She darted forward to kiss the stallion between the eyes.

He was too quick for her, of course. In a scuffle of hooves and a dusting of snow, he stepped back, but not far.

Head tilted to one side, the stallion looked with amused eyes through his thick white forelock. His nicker was like a chuckle as she moved away from him.

"Next time I'll be quicker," she promised. And when the stallion turned to go, so did she.

Sam made her way quickly through the tunnel, back to Ace and Jake.

As she did, she smiled. Part of her would always stay with the stallion, but she had two homes, two families. She was only leaving this one for a little while.

From

## Phantom Stallion

### GIFT HORSE

Next into the auction ring was the big draft horse named Tinkerbell.

The man who'd ridden the chestnut led Tinkerbell into the ring. He had to stretch to keep one hand on the rope clipped under the bay's chin, but the man had a knack with horses. Tinkerbell lifted his knees in a smooth trot. As the man ran to keep up, the big horse looked almost amused.

"Two hundred," Baldy called out.

"Two-fifty," said a young rancher in a plaid shirt. Unlike the others, he stood to make his bid.

"Three hundred," Baldy drawled lazily.

"Four-fifty." The young rancher had moved down the bleachers to stand beside the ring, as if pure want could win the horse for him.

"Five hundred," Baldy bid, then glanced at his notebook and, before the young rancher could make a counter offer, added, "Oh shoot, make it six."

"Six hundred," said the auctioneer. "Do I hear six-fifty?"

Sam's heart sank as the young rancher leaned forward on the arms he'd crossed on the top rail of the fence. He stared after Tinkerbell, then shook his head.

He was just being sensible, Sam knew. She recognized the look of surrender on his face, because
she'd seen it so often. A working rancher didn't
always get what he wanted, because the ranch always
came first.

"Going . . ."

Even if Dad had allowed her to use her reward
money, she couldn't have outbid Baldy. He saw the big
horse, who must weigh close to a ton, as pure profit.

Sam covered her eyes with both hands. All she
saw was a kind animal with the potential to do something grand.

"Going . . ."

Dad's hand felt warm against Sam's back, but she
kept her eyes closed. She wanted to stay in the darkness behind her eyelids. She could hear the thud of
the big animal's hooves, but she didn't have to watch
his trusting performance.

"Seven hundred," said Mr. Fairchild's crisp voice
over the microphone.

Sam looked up. Smiling through her tears, she
stared in the direction of the announcer's booth. It
was Mr. Fairchild. No one had bid against him for the
chestnut. Maybe it was a tradition to let him win.
Maybe he'd save Tinkerbell and sell him later to
someone who deserved him.

"Eight hundred," shouted Baldy.

No! Sam rocked forward, head down, as if she'd

been punched in the stomach. Tinkerbell had been so close to safety.

Boots shifted in the wooden stands. Dad gave a surprised grunt and everyone turned to stare at the man from Dagdown Packing Company.

"Bidding is closed at seven hundred dollars," the auctioneer said stiffly.

"I said eight hundred!" Baldy was standing now and his bare head had flushed red.

"That was our last horse of the day," the auctioneer went on, "and we at Mineral Auctions sure hope you folks will come back and see us next week."

"You wanna go see what Duke has in mind for that critter, I suppose," Dad said. He rose, stretched, and together he and Sam left the bleachers and started toward the holding pen.

She wanted to feel excited, but Baldy's dark presence lurked behind her.

Dad took longer strides than usual, and Sam was sure it was because he wanted to get her away from Baldy. The man was still shouting in the direction of the auctioneer's box.

"You can't ignore my bid!" he yelled.

But the auctioneer, who'd noticed the ranch woman's quiet bid on the pony, pretended not to hear.

"That's right," the auctioneer continued. "Every Thursday from ten 'til five, we're glad to have you as our guests. Drive safe, now."

As the microphone clicked off, Baldy stormed

toward the ring, looking furious. He paused when he came abreast of Sam and her dad. Sam shrank against Dad's side, but just to get out of the man's way.

Baldy was only a sore loser. There was nothing scary about that.

"I know what this is about," Baldy said in a threatening tone.

Dad stepped forward, making a wall between Sam and the man.

"Then maybe you'd better tell me," Dad said. His tone would sound lazy to anyone who didn't know him, but Sam could tell Baldy had made a mistake.

Dad was a protective father and Baldy's harsh expression was enough to provoke his anger.

Sam peered around Dad, trying to see Baldy's reaction.

He slapped his notebook against the side of his too-new jeans, and his eyes seemed to evaluate Dad in the same way he'd sized up the horses. Sam hoped the skinny man had figured out that Dad could snap him like a toothpick.

Baldy didn't look like he'd quite made up his mind about arguing, when he heard boots behind him and turned.

Mr. Fairchild straightened his gabardine coat to sit just so on his shoulders as he approached.

"We had a gentlemen's agreement," Baldy snapped.

In the moment of silence, Sam remembered Baldy

offering five hundred dollars for "the big boy" before the auction began. But Mr. Fairchild hadn't really said yes, had he?

"Guess that means I'm no gentleman," Mr. Fairchild responded, but Sam could tell he was saying something about Baldy, not himself.

"No, now, I'm not saying that."

"Then what are you saying?"

Baldy took a deep breath and shook his head. "Guess I'm saying I'll see you next week, Duke. Same time, same place." He started toward the parking lot, then stopped. "But I wanted that horse."

"If he's back here in a month, we'll talk," Mr. Fairchild said.

Sam felt another chill, which had nothing to do with the disappearance of the sun. The big horse wasn't safe yet. A paralyzing cold gripped the back of her neck.

"Fair enough," Baldy answered, nodding.

This time when he stamped toward the parking lot, he kept going.

Sam didn't watch him for long, because Mr. Fairchild turned toward her, rocked back a couple inches, and crossed his arms.

"As for you, young lady," he said, "I was mighty impressed with your little speech before the sales began. You weren't able to negotiate much with your father, but I'm wondering if we can work something out."

Sam could tell his words were partly aimed at Dad.

Dad took a deep breath, then released it in a sigh. When he didn't interrupt, Mr. Fairchild went on. "I'd be willing to go in partners with you on preparing that big bay brute for sale to someone who might make something of him. Would you be willing to do that?"

"Sure," Sam said, but her head spun. How could this be happening?

"First, I'll need a little earnest money." Mr. Fairchild rubbed his hands together. "You know what that is, don't you?"

"No sir," Sam admitted, "I don't."

"It means you give me enough cash, up front, so that I know you're serious, and that you'll keep your word."

To do what? Sam wondered, but she didn't ask. If she gave Mr. Fairchild more time to think, and Dad time to recover from his surprise, things might change.

"So reach down deep in that pocket of yours, young lady," Mr. Fairchild said. "And hope you come up with something."